DEAD WAIT

DEAD WAIT

Ferrel D. Moore

Mystery and Suspense Press
San Jose New York Lincoln Shanghai

Dead Wait

All Rights Reserved © 1997 by Ferrel D. Moore

No part of this book may be reproduced or transmitted in any form or by any means, graphic, electronic, or mechanical, including photocopying, recording, taping, or by any information storage retrieval system, without the permission in writing from the publisher.

Mystery and Suspense Press
an imprint of iUniverse, Inc.

For information address:
iUniverse, Inc.
5220 S. 16th St., Suite 200
Lincoln, NE 68512
www.iuniverse.com

Any similiarities between the fictional characters in Dead Wait and real life persons are strictly coincidental.

ISBN: 0-595-21113-5

Printed in the United States of America

Contents

Chapter 1 1
Chapter 2 19
Chapter 3 33
Chapter 4 49
Chapter 5 63
Chapter 6 79
Chapter 7 91
Chapter 8 101
Chapter 9 115
Chapter 10 131
Chapter 11 143
Chapter 12 153
Chapter 13 165
Chapter 14 175

CHAPTER 1

I would have killed him myself if they hadn't beaten me to it, but I would have done it with my bare hands. He had, after all, let my sister die.

The article in the Sunday paper detailing my best friend Davey Wiltz' death came out Saturday night—if you wanted the edition without the comics. I didn't read about it until Sunday, since, as I matter of preference, I get the Sunday paper delivered to my house on Sunday. The last thing that the doctor had told me after I had been institutionalized and as I was being released was that I needed a simple, ordered life. Little routines, he had suggested, could make me feel like I was a normal person instead of a head case. That's not exactly what he said; I'm paraphrasing it a bit. But I'm better now, honest.

The doctor, whom Lydia Retkin had arranged for, had advised me against watching television or movies with violent content, and had even told me to stay from newspapers and books with violence in them. He had given me lots of pills and prescriptions that I promised to take. I don't lie much, but I did what I had to do to get out. I wasn't comfortable being restrained.

There was another bit of psychiatric advice that I had had trouble following, and that was to cultivate normal friends. I just didn't know how. I tried explaining it to the doctor, but he kept insisting that making normal friends was like learning how to ride a bike—you fell down sometimes, but once learned you could never really forget the technique. I had never fallen off of my bike as a kid, but I had pushed a lot of other kids off of theirs.

Davey Wiltz had been my first and only attempt at making a normal friend. Davey wasn't normal, but, as far as I known at the time, he hadn't killed anyone, so I think that the doctor would have approved. If I had ever gone back to see the doctor for my follow up appointments, I could have asked him what he thought. As it was, I just settled on Davey as my best and only friend.

In addition to being my best friend, up until the moment that I found out about what he had done to my sister, Davey was the fattest man that I have ever known. He sweated constantly, but never seemed to shed a pound. His shirts were like water rags that had to be twisted and squeezed every now and then to keep him from looking like he just got out of the swimming pool. The water loss alone should have shaved off a few kilograms, but his body didn't seem to pay much attention to the laws of nature—gravity included. Davey himself didn't seem to care much for the social laws that other people live by—since he made his living sucking money from unsuspecting marks via elaborate scams—but, up until the night that I had decided to kill him, he had been my best friend, so I let it slide.

The RCMP was investigating the matter, according to the paper, since, although Davey was an American citizen, the murder had occurred on Canada. The U.S. authorities would be involved as well, et cetera, et cetera. The killer or killers were still at large, and, from what I could tell, the Canadian police didn't have a clue as to who they were.

Par for the course.

The Sunday paper had also said that Davey had been shot in the heart. It was kind of ironic, considering the problems that he had been having with his pseudo-girlfriend Vickie.

The two of them weren't going anywhere anyway, in my opinion. Together, they weighed in at four hundred and thirty eight pounds, with Davey accounting for four hundred and forty two of that total. He could have hurt her in bed, if they had ever ended up there.

Maybe you think that I'm being an asshole for pointing that out, especially since he was now officially out of breath, but friendship, like rank, has its own privileges.

I never knew what he saw in her, though. Except for her looks and her body, she was a total zero. Wide eyes, lipstick ad quality lips, and elegant bone structure—that's what I remember about her face. Her hair was long, and was a pants-stirring mixture of honey blond accented with light brown streaks. When she French-braided it, she was so pretty that usually I tried not to look at her. She was, after all, Davey's girlfriend, not mine.

To make matters worse for Davey, Vickie Matisse was only five feet tall; a thin, slight shadow frequently lost in the shade of Davey's mountainous bulk. Davey was painfully aware of the visuals, the eye-jarring contrast between their respective sizes.

During our last phone conversation, when he called me on his car phone roughly three hours before he died, he was actually crying about his relationship with her. He had been telling me that he had come to the conclusion that although a woman as beautiful as Vickie could have a man as grossly overweight as him for a friend, she could never really love him. Blubbering might be more accurate. When Dave cried, he did so with tremulous heaves and dramatic gasps that were usually a "4" on the Richter scale. He blubbered easily and frequently—usually about the stupidest things.

He blubbered two years ago when, leaving a chess tournament in downtown Detroit, the two of us had seen the old black lady in the pink Cadillac run the stoplight and kill the tattooed biker on his screaming black and chrome Harley at the intersection of Woodward and Fort.

The impact had thrown the body thirty feet or so to land on the sidewalk in front of us with a sickening liquid crunch like the sound of a hard-shelled insect breaking beneath your shoe.

Another dope-dealing biker dead was the way that I had figured it. Why should it matter to me? It wasn't a pleasant thing to witness up close, but I wasn't going to lose any sleep over it. I had seen worse in Viet Nam.

Davey saw it differently. He had broken down about it right there on the sidewalk in front of the other witnesses, dropping his elephantine bulk forward and onto his knees to weep as though the biker had been a relative, or a dues-paying, card-carrying human being at the very least.

The old white woman standing three feet to left of where the biker's body had landed agreed with my attitude. "Take that, you little prick," she had said. She had stopped short of kicking the body once for good measure.

Different points of view, I guess. Davey felt torment; the old white lady and I were rooting for the driver of the Cadillac. I suppose that, as alien as Davey's feelings were to me, it was one of the main reasons that we had been friends. Unlike myself, Davey at least had emotions. Being around him at least allowed me to experience human feelings vicariously. When you've done the kind of things that I've done in my life, you need emotional reinforcement occasionally. To me, the biker was dead and that was that.

It was difficult for me to understand why Davey could not appreciate the sweet irony of the street gangster's death. This biker was white, extra-large with a bloated potbelly, and even his darkly mirrored sunglasses added to the tough-guy effect. He had had a long, black and gray braided ponytail sticking out from under his helmet, and a blue swastika tattooed on his left cheek. The words "Iron Spike" were sewn onto the back of his black leather jacket. I remember that his bike had bounced and landed upside down, with the engine still cranking away making throaty Harley thunder.

He had come at his side of the intersection on his Harley roaring mean and full of bad attitude, the way a Wild West outlaw must have come riding into Dodge City. He was tough and he knew it, but he was about to learn a lesson about tough.

The little old black lady had come at her side of the intersection driving thirty-five miles an hour. She would have noticed the light turning red, she said later, if she hadn't dropped her purse on the floor and reached over to grab it.

A little old lady looking for her purse on a robin's egg blue day had killed iron Spike. I had felt good about it, but Davey had blubbered over the guy. Every human being had something good in them, according to Davey. That was what made him such a good con artist, I suppose. He could cry over a total stranger. He had been born with a double share of empathy.

Davey's emoting wasn't for show, either. A lot of people have allergies. They're sensitive to dust, or flowers, or cats or dogs or whatever. Davey was, I believe, sensitive to life.

It worked to his advantage when he was running a con on a mark. He identified with them completely, even while he was relieving them of their money. He actually believed his cons were legitimate business.

It was also why he was so guilt ridden afterwards. He was the only con artist I ever knew who called the marks back afterwards to apologize. Davey was a mess. But he was my friend.

Davey hadn't always been a con—he was a late entry to the field. He had been a computer programmer for years. He used to say that all that time sitting on his but in front of a monitor eating potato chips was responsible for his weight problem. He had some kind of a wrist problem called carpal tunnel syndrome or something like that forced him out of programming and when he found that no one wanted to hire someone his size, he had turned to scamming money any way that he could.

I can't really say why I hadn't killed him a long time ago, though, when he ran a con on me the first time that we met. He had conned me into buying a hundred thousand dollars worth of ruby that turned out to be synthetic material roughed up in a Laundromat drier to look like rough stones out of Burma. It was a good enough job that it fooled the jeweler I had had examine them. I found out later that Davey had kicked him back fifty to temporarily cloud his judgment.

What really torqued my nuts too tight, however, was the fact that I was buying the ruby for someone else as a favor, and that I had done some digging around to find Davey. In other words, I was counting on Davey, whom I didn't know well at that point, to deliver the goods because I didn't know shit about precious stones. The man that I was buying them for knew a lot more than I did, and informed me that I had been taken. He wasn't about to pay for counterfeit, which meant that I was out the money.

So when Davey called me back to apologize, I should have tracked him down and shot him right then. He had cost me money and fair share of embarrassment. Also, it would have saved me time later, and someone else wouldn't have beaten me to it. But, like so many of Davey's marks, I let it ride. I can't say why. It was just hard to stay pissed at such an emotional guy. He was genuinely remorseful that he had sold me counterfeit. For some reason that I can't really explain, I wound up consoling him, I think, telling him that it wasn't his fault. If I hadn't been reformed by that time, though, he would have been dead. Maybe I was trying to prove to myself that I was a different man than I used to be.

Davey gave me back some of the cash later—about half of what was left, I think. That's another thing that I can't explain; I didn't need the money enough to think about it too much.

The newspaper said that Davey was whacked within three hours of when I talked to him, at about eleven o'clock Saturday night. He was shot getting out of his car in a Holiday Inn parking lot in Toronto. A target that big must have been hard to miss, even at night.

As I read about it in the Sunday paper, I took it like I took anybody's death since my sister's—it happens, it's over. Nobody else seemed to count much after that. I worry about myself sometimes—not too much, but enough. When my sister died, I went to her house every night for a month after she was buried. I sat across the street in my car, the engine running, and the lights off. The police got used to me sitting there. The first night, though, they tried to roust me. They were pretty rough until my story checked out. Then they let me return to my vigil. I could see it in their eyes, though. They thought that I was a very sick puppy.

At night, anything could happen; that was the way that I looked at it. I admit that I was a little nuts. I wasn't as bad as when they institutionalized me, but I was getting there for a while after her death.

We had buried my sister Diedre, but a part of me figured that if I waited there long enough every night, she eventually just might show up to check on her house. It never happened, of course, but I waited anyway.

She was twenty-six when she had died in a diabetic coma in her own living room. On the night that he had died, Davey told me over his car phone that he had been with my sister and watched her die; that he had in fact kept her from her medication. He was sorry, he said, so very sorry. Could I ever forgive him? I couldn't hear the rest of what he said over the next few minutes because my brain was on overload. He might have been explaining the reasons why he didn't give her the medicine that she needed. I'll never know. I didn't listen to what he was saying. I had already made up my mind to kill him.

It was a rational decision on my part. I wasn't over the edge. My thoughts were hot with anger, but not parboiled, and I hadn't heard the voice of the Dark Judge like I did before. The doctors had said that the Dark Judge was my subconscious guilt for something that I had done that they could never peg coming through in the form of an audible voice. It sounded good, but, although doctors usually mean well, they didn't know much about the haunted caverns of the mind where demon voices echo through the passageways of fear that God has tunneled through our brains.

Before going to bed that night, after the fire in my mind had burned to dull embers, it occurred to me that the two events—Davey's death and my sister's—were separated by eleven days short of five years.

Davey, had done a lot of good things for her and me in the intervening five years, but I still would have killed him, if someone hadn't already beaten me to it. By not giving her medication at a crucial moment, you see, I thought that Davey had effectively murdered her.

What goes around comes back around.

Eventually.

I lived in a house in Detroit in what used to be a very, very expensive neighborhood. If I had to sell the place now, if it was still standing, that is, I don't think that I would even recoup half of the amount of money that I spent improving it with all of the high tech devices that I could get my hands on. Detroit housing on Indian Trail has taken a steady dive over the last fifteen years.

My house was alarmed and barred like a bank in a bad neighborhood. I had video cameras that watched other video cameras, and a computer in my den that watched them all. The man who had lived in the place before me had installed a bomb shelter and explosion proof elevator in the center of the house. You good quality security arrangements, at least, when you buy from a drug dealer. Occasionally, to show that I'm not paranoid about the way the neighborhood has degenerated, I leave the back door unlocked. I don't do that anymore.

The cleaning ladies come weekly, but it's not like I give a shit how the place looks. I just like the company. If you want to feel really alone, try living in ten thousand square feet of house by yourself. Every now and then I feel like yelling "hello" to see if anyone else is home.

It was Sunday, and I had just finished throwing the paper with the story on Davey's death into the trash. I was the only one home except for Mrs. Alderton, the live-in tenant that Lydia had sent to me who was going on sixty-eight years old—just so that you don't get the wrong idea. Mrs. Alderton had lived with me for the last five years. The company was nice.

It was nine thirty, and the sun was already too bright for me. April in Michigan is a good month. They say that in California it stays like Michigan in April all year round. Personally, I'd find that a little boring. Then again, look what it does to the brains of people living on the West coast. It may get a little cold in Michigan during the winter, but I think I'll stay right where I'm at.

If I really wanted to improve my lifestyle, I suppose that I could have moved out of Detroit. New scenery that you didn't have to look out through bars to see might be nice, but I didn't think that Lydia would have let me. She liked me where I could be watched.

But I would still be alone, not counting old Mrs. Alderton, so what would be the point?

Even fat Davey had a woman. Maybe I'd get one for myself someday. Maybe that would make the scenery a little easier to take.

Somebody had to tell Vickie the news. I couldn't think of any reason to deny myself the pleasure. The question of who had actually killed Davey and why never even occurred to me until I was well on my way to Vicki's. I would have thought about it sooner, I suppose, if the gasman hadn't tried to kill me.

It was a classic.
The doorbell rang.
I ignored it the way that I usually do.
The doorbell rang again.

I got out of my chair and stretched. It was Sunday morning, and I really only had three or people that knew where I lived. I was careful about that. Even though I'm effectively retired, I had a lot of enemies with long memories and strong resources who didn't really give a shit if I'd had a grand mal nervous breakdown. They would still enjoy hurting me. I had parted with them on bad terms, and they wanted to even the score. Most of my problems in this area come from my philosophy that you should not only burn your bridges behind you, you should also napalm anyone on them at the time. That's what the Dark Judge had advised me. That was when I had done the Bad Thing.

What I used to do before I had been retired was contract enforcement for Lydia Retkin. She would send me in to protect her side of a deal; I would take care of business. Usually, things went the way that she had planned, and nothing got out of hand. Sometimes it got a little more complicated.

You know the way that the rich are; they never have enough money, so sooner or later they start getting involved with people and situations that they shouldn't be dicking with at all.

Lydia had the looks, the money, and the power. If you want to get picky about it, she was too good looking, had way too much money and power for her own good, and liked to get in way over her head because if she wasn't involved in something risky or at the very least sordid, she got bored. Lydia Retkin didn't like to be bored, and with her kind of money she could and did stir up some real shit.

I didn't really care; she paid me well for what I did. I made enemies along the way working for her, but like I said, she paid me well. I just had to make sure that I watched out for myself.

Which is why I checked the monitor in the study before going anywhere near the door. I saw a trim, average looking young man with a rough mess of brown hair. He wore a name patch on one breast that said job, another on the opposite side that Union Gas Company. Bob's lips were too thin, his expression too alert, and his face too happy to be a real employee. What employee in their right mind would be happy about working on a Sunday?

I had metal detectors built into the pillars outside the door. They weren't alarming, but metal detectors are sort of outmoded in these days of high strength composite plastics.

Bob rang the doorbell again.

I was getting pissed.

He wasn't for real, that's what my guts told me.

Hit man? Not likely, I thought. What self-respecting hit-person dresses like the gasman? That would be too embarrassing.

Still, he definitely wasn't the gasman.

I pegged his age at or about twenty-three. In another age, it would be young for a hired killer. He was maybe five feet ten, around one hundred and seventy pounds. His hands looked to be not too rough, but then again, gas men and guns-for-hire don't really work all that much or all that often.

I pressed the intercom button on the desk.

"You want something?" I asked.

I didn't want to tip him off by sounding too nice on a Sunday morning. He'd know that I was on to him—nobody is happy being interrupted before noon on Sunday.

"Is this Mr. Sulu?" he asked in an eager, almost boyishly high-pitched voice.

I had the nine-millimeter out of the drawer, could feel it's reassuring weight in my hand. A nine mil isn't a forty-five, but it gets the job done, believe me.

"Who's asking?"

While I was playing games with gas-boy, two of them were out back preparing to blast their way in. If I weren't retired, maybe I would have figured that out before they got into the house.

I pushed the intercom button again.

"Who's asking?"

"We've got reports of a gas leak in the area, Mr. Sulu. This is Mr. Sulu, isn't it?"

"And who are you?"

"I'm with the gas company, sir."

"Sure you are," I said. "There's no gas leak here, so keep moving."

"I can't do that. I've got to have you sign this form first."

They were in the back door by that time, although I didn't figure that out until later. Two of them, armed with the same gun that I was carrying, creeping through my kitchen door, and I didn't have a clue. It's embarrassing to look back on. I was lucky to live through it. If it hadn't been for Mrs. Alderton, I wouldn't be telling this story.

She backed into the kitchen carrying a wad of kitchen towels and surprised the two just as they passed the kitchen table. Gray haired little old ladies don't exactly intimidate professional killers, so when she turned to face them, the first, a round faced little prick whose name we never did find out, took his time raising his pistol to plug her.

I heard the shot from the study—from her gun, not his. She fired through the stack of towels and caught him clean in the face with a round. I don't know if you've ever seen anyone take a bullet in the face, and I don't know if I even want to describe it to you, so let me just say that his head sprayed a lot of brain and blood all over my kitchen.

She turned and shot the second gunman in the throat. Same result. Later, she told me that he was too pretty to shoot in the face. I'd never asked Mrs. Alderton about her sex life. She seemed a little old to me to be sizing up young men by how good looking they were before she shot them.

"Clear," I heard her yell.

It caught me in mid-stride.

"Clear?" I yelled back.

"That's what I said," she snapped back.

"Yes, ma'am," I said under my breath.

I returned to the desk and looked at the monitor. Young Bob was looking a little nervous.

It was a judgment call. I could have done a lot of things, but what I did was go downstairs, open the door, and shoot him in the knee before he could go for his gun.

He was screaming bloody murder as I dragged him inside and dumped him onto the ceramic tiled floor. I think that it was his first time taking a bullet. Veterans don't cry and thrash around the floor aimlessly. We've got other moves. I think we even bleed better.

"Don't worry about the noise," I told him as I relieved him of his weapon, which he carried, of all places, in his back pocket. "People around here are used to it. A day without a gunshot in this neighborhood is like a day without pollution."

"You fucker," he screamed.

"Mrs. Alderton doesn't like bad language," I advised him, "and since she just wasted your friend in the kitchen, I'd watch my mouth if I were you."

"Friends. Two of them," corrected Mrs. Alderton as she came up behind me. "Two more fine pieces of man-flesh dead. What a waste. On a Sunday, of all things. I'm going straight to hell."

I turned and flashed her a grin.

"Keep your eye on the mark," she said irritably.

She was five feet, five inches tall, when she didn't stoop. Her hair was blue-gray enough meet the AARP specs for old people. She was wrinkled in the appropriate places, had two liver spots on the back of her left hand that she absolutely hated, but her eyes were still as blue and hard as my own. I never knew my mother, but I fantasized that she was something like Mrs. Alderton.

"You're dead, man, you're dead," moaned Young Bob.

Mrs. Alderton crouched down near the youngster's head as though to hear him better. Her dress slid up so that it was just under her knees, and I got a frightening glimpse of the canvas colored, high tensile strength nylons that old women wear.

"Young man," she said, trying to get his attention.

"Fuck, fuck, fuck," screamed Young Bob.

She looked up at me, sighed, turned back and jammed the barrel of her gun in his mouth. His eyes popped wide, as though someone had pulled a string on the back of his head.

"You need to learn some manners," she counseled him softly.

"Umgle-rrgle," he replied.

"Don't talk with your mouth full," I said.

"I have a touch of arthritis in my knees," she continued, "and I don't like to bend down. Do you understand? Just nod your head slowly if you do."

He did. His head inclined once, very slowly.

"Your mother has the same problem, I'll bet, doesn't she?"

Young Bob inclined once again. I was betting that he didn't have a mother.

"Now, you're bleeding all over Mr. Sulu's nice floor, dear. But after all, you and your friends were trying to kill us on a Sunday. Fair's fair, don't you think?

Young Bob just wasn't getting her humor. His eyes were starting to glass over, and I could smell that he'd pissed his pants.

"Just kill him," I said.

Wide went the eyes again, and his head moved slowly side to side, so as not to tick off Mrs. Alderton. Sweat was beaded on his forehead, and his skin was a gray color. His light blue pant leg was soaked in blood. It pooled and spread on the floor. I'd hit something important when I shot him.

His eyelids fluttered, and the pupils rolled back.

Mrs. Alderton saw it, and gently pulled the barrel out of the kid's mouth. She straightened painfully and looked up at me with a hard stare.

"What?" I asked defensively. "You never wanted to shoot a meter man?"

I left Mrs. Alderton to clean up the blood and get rid of the body. She had a lot of experience in those areas. A quick phone call and a van would pull up at the house carrying a roll of carpet. They would leave carrying the same carpet, with Young Bob rolled inside. The blood—well, Mrs. Alderton knew how to get rid of blood. When the team left, everything would be spic and span.

Mrs. Alderton would watch them through her seamless bifocals, looking up over her little bird's beak of a nose, taking care of business. In her prime, she must have been hell to cross. She had worked for most of her life in some government agency that she rarely talked about. If I was her kid and she told me to clean my room, I'd have done it right away.

Lydia Retkin had introduced us a few weeks before I had retired. I figured it was Lydia's way of looking out for me or spying on me—one or the other. I didn't really care which after a while. It was nice having the old lady around. She was a good shot.

Vickie was wearing a black elastic exercise outfit when she opened the door to let me in. I had never been to her apartment before. Under other circumstances, I might have felt awkward just showing up.

"I need to talk to you," I said.

She looked at me with a vacant stare for a moment, and then let me in. I wondered what was going through her mind. My own thoughts were a little out of line for the moment; it's hard to ignore a good-looking woman in tight exercise clothes no matter what the situation. Her honey-blond hair was tied back in a ponytail, and a thin film of sweat covered her forearms. A white towel was draped around her neck and over her shoulders. She had been pedaling on a stationary bike that sat across the room next to the window and in front of her television. The VCR play light was lit and a movie about space aliens was playing out on the television.

Vickie pointed me to a chair and plopped back on her couch, her head leaning back against the cushions, her legs splayed apart.

"How many miles?" I asked.

She exhaled hard through her slightly parted lips as though to blow an offending hair away. There's nothing quite like watching a woman in black elastic breathe.

"Ten—so far," she replied.

"You do this every morning?"

"Five miles every week day, ten on Saturdays and Sunday."

"Brutal schedule," I said.

She was watching me with more interest than she usually showed. I had changed clothes before I left, so it wasn't like she was looking at a blood spot that I had missed.

"So why are you here?" she asked.

It had seemed like a good idea at the time to come over and tell her in person. I never liked Vickie, she reminded me too much of my ex-wife. It wasn't her fault, but it bothered me anyway. Laurie, my ex, had been in bed with the gasman when I came home unexpectedly one day. Now you know why I don't much care for utility workers. He had looked, come to think about it, a little like Young Bob.

"It's about Davey," I said.

"Oh."

"He's dead, Vickie."

"I need a cigarette," she said.

"I said he's dead.

"I heard you the first time," she said with an edge to her voice. She looked toward the window, and exhaled again, but did not re-inflate. Her shoulders slumped forward and her eyes began to mist.

I leaned forward a little, waiting for the full-blown waterworks to begin.

"How'd he die?" she finally asked.

Her voice was as flat as plate glass.

"Someone shot him."

"Why?"

It was a good question.

"I don't know."

"Who did it?"

"I don't know that either."

The noonday sun filled the room with bright light. April is a pretty month, even in Detroit. Outside, trees had green leaves, flowers bloomed bright colors, and the air was slightly cool. Her window was open, and a fresh breeze blew in through the screen. The sound was off on the television, but I saw an alien explode into a violent, putrescent mess.

"He was on his cell phone to me a few hours before it happened," added.

"How'd you find out?" she asked.

"Morning paper," I said.

"What are you going to do about it?"

"What do you mean?"

Her eyes fastened on me, and I felt a hard rage behind them.

"He was your friend. Are you going to let someone shoot him and get away with it?"

"Do I look like a cop?" I asked.

She didn't answer.

"What do you want me to do?"

I didn't tell her about the way that Dave had let my sister die. It was none of her business.

"He was your friend," she persisted.

"The police will take care of it—the RCMP, since he was an American."

"What?"

"He was killed in Toronto," I explained patiently.

"Why?"

"I already told you that I don't know."

"No, I mean do you know why was he in Toronto?"

Another good question. But from the look in her eyes, I thought that she already knew why he was in Toronto, but for some reason wanted to see if I knew, too.

"Look, Vickie, I don't know much of anything. I just didn't want you to read about it in the papers, that's all."

She hadn't taken her eyes from mine. We hadn't had so much eye contact in the entire time that I had known her.

"Find out."

"It's not my job. Don't get all gagged out on me. He's dead, I don't know why, and I don't know who, and it's done and over."

I almost told her that we couldn't bring him back, but I was already exceeding the cliché speed limit.

"Don't you care?" she asked.

She was full of good questions that day.

That night, I dreamed that I sat in a courtroom with wainscoted walls and a ceiling fan going round and round and round to circulate the dead air that precedes judgment.

A dark, hooded figure sat on the elevated bench, and a skeleton motioned for me to rise and receive my sentence. My knees were weak as I stood, and, as always, I looked peered at the Dark Judge's cowl to see his face, but saw only blackness instead.

It had been a juryless trial.

"You," the Dark Judge echoed, "will seek and destroy the murderer of Davey Wiltz, and then," he added, "you will end your own evil life. The weight of your soul will be lightened, and you will die purified."

"May I speak in my own defense?" I inquired.

"Guilty until proven innocent," whispered the Dark Judge.

CHAPTER 2

"Nice look," said Billy Bumper.

"So what'd you find out?" I asked.

We were in a mall restaurant, eating some kind of Mexican shit. I was wearing my herringbone jacket, a crème colored open necked shirt, and faded jeans. Billy was sipping a margarita; I was having my usual black coffee. My meeting with Vickie had decided me that I should look into what happened to Davey. My dream had nothing to do with it. In the course of things, I thought that I might learn something more about his relationship with my sister. If it turned out that he had just let her die for no justifiable reason, then to hell with him and good luck to whoever shot him. If not, then Vickie was right. He was my friend and I should even the score with his murderer or murderers. It wasn't my normal line of work, but, then, it was really a personal matter and I would do what I could.

"Can't you get a new coat?" grinned Billy.

"I like this coat," I said.

"It needs to be put to sleep."

"You need to be put to sleep."

"Hey," said Billy, rearing back in his chair, "that's not funny."

"No offense. Now, what did you find out?"

Billy shoved back his glasses, and got a dab of guacamole on the bridge. "I don't like hearing that kind of stuff. You know I got a weak heart. You say something like that to me, and I could be gone, just like that."

He snapped his fingers to emphasize the point. They made a muffled sound, like a dud firecracker.

"Yeah, well, it was sarcasm. You familiar with the word?"

"You know," he said, "I help you out and you abuse me."

"You haven't told me anything yet," I pointed out.

"I was hungry," he said. "You think that I could get another of these things?" He held up the last of his chimichanga and then shoved it into his mouth. "But I got something for you, yeah I did."

Billy was a smart little man, but I hated dealing with him. I was paying him big bucks for the information; you'd think that he could buy his own damned lunch.

"What'd you get?"

Billy reached over and took a taco chip from the bowl. His sleeve scooped a blob of sour cream from a dish. Sooner or later it would end up on his pants. I didn't bother to enlighten him.

He wasn't much to look at, as his type went. Little tufts of brown hair dotted his forehead as though he were in the process of receiving hair transplants. His face was flat, and slightly concave. There was a touch of gray in his overlong sideburns. Elvis he was not. Billy's shoulders were narrow, he had a slight paunch, and his fingers, well, they were two damn feminine. On his right hand, I saw his prized high school ring. It was the ugliest school ring that I have ever seen. He looked like a sissy.

"You were the last call he made on his cell phone."

"Thanks for nothing," I grumbled.

"Whoa, partner, there's more. Just hang on to your saddle horn."

"Quit talking like that, you sound like a queer."

"I'm not a queer," he said. "I've got a wife and two brats."

"Louder," I told him. "Let the rest of the restaurant in on your secret." His eyes darted around the room like a small squirrel's would if it were looking for acorns. Nobody, he found, was paying him the slightest bit of attention.

"You're an asshole, Jason," he said.

"Don't I know it? Now, what else did you find?"

"I don't know if I should tell you now. I could get in a lot of trouble if anybody found out what I was doing for you."

"Little late to get a conscience, isn't it?" I asked.

"I've got to look out for myself."

"Would you just fucking tell me?"

"All right, all right. You were the last person that he called, but your call was interrupted. Right?"

"We got cut off," I explained. "He probably drove by some power lines."

"No way," said Billy shaking his head. "You were cut off by another customer on a cell phone. Davey was linked to another cell phone call in progress by mistake."

"I don't understand," I said. "Do you mean that he wound up talking to someone else?"

"Yep," said Billy, "it happens sometimes."

"You ought to be ashamed to work for the phone company."

"It's a living."

"It's a great front for shopping their databases for cash prizes," I told him.

"Hey, you want to know who he wound up talking to, or do you want to keep being a prick?"

Billy loved it when he talked tough.

"Who?" I asked.

"You're going to love this."

"So tell me.

"He cut in on this phone call between this guy calling from his car and Traxor."

"Traxor?" I asked. "What in the hell is a Traxor?"

"Don't you read the papers?"

"Apparently not enough," I said.

"The place that blew up on Monday at four in the morning. One of their main scientists and a security guard died. Jesus, it was all over television and everything…"

"Let me get this straight. Davey gets accidentally patched into a conversation somebody's having with somebody else at Traxor, Davey gets wasted three hours later, and the very next day the place is incinerated?"

"Yeah," he grinned. "Some coincidence, eh?"

"Yeah," I agreed, "that's some coincidence."

It was Wednesday.

I hadn't talked to Vickie since Sunday when I had dropped the dime on her.

When I left the Mexican restaurant, I had two names and addresses in my pocket to think about in addition to what Vickie had said. I couldn't get her out of my mind. That had always been the problem. She annoyed me. There was something about her, but I wasn't really attracted to her, other than her looks. She knew who I was. She knew what I was. Davey had told her, I was deadass certain of that. Yet in all of the time that I had known her, she hadn't said a word. My guess was that with a father like Nat Matisse, someone like me was the least of her worries.

Actually, to be honest about it, the mystery of who she was and what she and Davey were to each other was eating at me a bit more than the question of who had killed Davey and why.

There was really no percentage in following up Davey's death. Like I said, I would have killed him myself if they hadn't beaten me to it. But it was starting to nag at me that I hadn't listened to Davey's explanation—what there was of it before we got cut off. I hate cellular phones. All I had listened to was my old self, the one that used to kill people when I was paid to do it or when the Dark Judge demanded it.

Don't get me wrong. I don't go around randomly killing people. You have to understand that he had stood by and watched my sister die. My sister. The one who never hurt anybody. Why had he done that? A new career in assisted suicide? It didn't make sense. The more that I thought about it, the less sense that it made.

Diedre had been a mess before she died. Her mind was worse off than her body. She had been constantly in and out of "relationships", and always with slugs. They always had girlfriends, or were married, or just plain assholes. She was a good-looking lady. I guess it's tough for beautiful women. Everybody wants them. Which, I guess, explained the mixed feelings I had about Vickie.

Diedre didn't work, not really. She did "artistic consulting" for corporate types. There are a lot of sharks in those waters, and she got eaten by most of them, so to speak.

Mostly she would match their office furniture and paintings to their personality type, which she decided using some kind of color charting and handwriting analysis, with a little astrology thrown in for good measure. She was a little flaky if you evaluated her objectively, but she was a good soul and never hurt anybody. You can't ask much more than that of a person.

Now she was dead. No more corporate bullshit for her.

The question was, why had Davey let her die?

The only reason I had used Billy Bumper was that I had decided to find out as much about Davey as I could. Maybe then I would understand why he let her die. I'm not saying that it would exonerate him, but at least I could rest a little easier. Which was why when I left the restaurant, I headed to Davey's house. If I tossed the place, maybe I could find something that would help me piece the puzzle together. If that didn't work, I'd drop by Anita's, Billy's perennial rival in the information tracking business, and see if she could ferret something out for me.

As I drove to Plymouth, which is the town where Davey lived, it occurred to me that within a day of Davey's death, three men had showed up at my place to kill me. The chances of there being a connection were slim, but it was a fact that two out of the four parties that had been on the phone with Davey that night were eliminated. Davey was dead. Traxor and whoever was in it at the time of the explosion were dead, and someone had tried to take me out. If they had succeeded, that would have meant that three out of four would have been taken care of. That was a pretty big coincidence.

I called Mrs. Alderton on my car phone to tell her what I was thinking. She listened without interruption—she was good at that.

"So what do you plan on doing about it, dear?" she asked.

"I'm on my way to Davey's place now to see if I can find out what kind of a scam he was running. Maybe he was floating a con and got killed for it."

"And you think that whoever shot him thinks that you were involved?"

"No," I told her, "I think that whoever killed him could have tracked me down by using someone like Billy Bumper to loot the phone company's phone records data base."

"Well, you'll be home for dinner, won't you?"

"Most likely. This won't take too long. Did you get the place cleaned up?"

"Does the Pope where a wild looking hat?"

"I'll take that as a yes."

"Naturally, dear."

"Well, you be careful, Lucy."

"Always."

"And try not to shoot any innocent bystanders."

"Watch your mouth."

"Yes, ma'am," I said. "Bye for now."

The phone was encrypted, so I wasn't worried about an intercept, but she was right, of course. It was careless of me to mention shooting over the phone. I'd been retired for only a few years, and already I was slipping.

"What a pig pen," I said under my breath.

Davey should never been allowed to live in Plymouth. It was a haven for upscale people who didn't allow dust in their homes. It was too neat, clean, orderly, and too well planned a town for a pig like Davey to be allowed to have his trough in their yuppie theme park.

I got in easily enough. Davey's home had an expensive security system, but it was commercial. He might as well have left the door open for me.

He lived on the edge of the city limits in a colonial house that stood alone on an otherwise vacant street, so I didn't have neighbors to worry about.

Inside, the living room was a cluttered, tossed mess. Someone else had been there before me. Someone messier than Davey.

"Davey, Davey," I said out loud, "who in the world did you piss off?"

No answer.

Whoever had done the toss job obviously didn't care whether or not anyone knew that the place had been searched. Pictures from the wall were broken, and the backs ripped out. Davey collected pen and inks from unknown artists. He had a couple on the walls of every room in the house, including quite a few in the bathroom. He spent a lot of time there.

You eat a lot you shit a lot.

Davey's rare book collection was scattered throughout the floor, the bookcase was overturned on top of them, the drawers looked to have been thrown against a wall and smashed into splinters.

I felt a chill pass over me, and looked toward a window. A hazy form hovered there as though watching me. The Dark Judge had sent a Dark Flunky to check up on me.

"I'm doing my job," I announced.

The Dark Flunky faded away.

I knew that it was only my mind playing tricks on me, but since the same could be said of life in general, I returned to checking out the mess.

There was no opened secret wall safe, nothing specific that pointed me in the right direction as to what the intruders had been looking for. What was more frustrating was that if they had found what they had wanted and had taken it, I would never know. I had been to Davey's house only rarely.

The chance that what they had been looking for was right out in the opened faded quickly. I didn't think that I was dealing with a Purloined Letter situation.

I was looking for something different, something that would tip me off as to why Davey had been in Toronto. Maybe a new painting or a mysterious package. Something with the word "clue" stenciled on it in bright red letters.

It didn't make sense. Davey had been accidentally switched into a phone call. That's what Billy Bumper had told me, and Billy ought to know. Therefore whomever he had been patched into should have been total strangers. What could they be looking for in his house?

What if I was reading the whole thing wrong, though? What if Davey hadn't been killed by total strangers, but by a mutual acquaintance of ours who had a reason to come after us both?

I wasn't a detective. Trying to think like one was giving me a headache. And with the place totally destroyed, how in the hell was I supposed to get a clue as to what these people had been looking for?

Each of the rooms was a disaster. The kitchen, Davey's home away from home, was the worst. Boxes had been taken from shelves, and their contents dumped on the floor. Toasty-O's cereal crunched underneath my feet as I gave it the once over. The floor and sugar containers had been poured into the sink. What a frigging mess.

Maybe there wasn't anything they were looking for. Maybe they were just trying to make it look like there was something that they were looking for. Maybe, maybe, maybe...

God, I hated looking for clues. I was a retired contract enforcer, not a detective. So far, the only thing that I had noticed was that Davey's computer was missing from his den. That didn't do me much good. It was a laptop, anyway; he could have taken it with him to Toronto. If he had done that, the RCMP would have it in lock up. I made a mental note to check that out.

If the toss-team had taken it from his house, I was shit out of luck. Whatever had been the hard drive was gone, and I didn't consider that much help. If I had found his computer, maybe I could have located a Cyber Clue or two.

Another maybe occurred to me. Maybe one group had whacked Davey, and another had tossed his place looking for whatever they thought that he had been hiding. It was possible that the two were in fact unconnected.

Yeah, sure.

I was in the hallway that led straight from the kitchen to the front door when I heard a car pull up. It was just what I needed, unless, of course, it was the police. Looking out the window would be stone cold stupid, however, so I stepped quickly into the living room and flattened against the wall that was recessed three feet from the entrance.

That was the other problem with looking for clues; every time you were just getting into it, someone showed up to interrupt.

My car was around the back, out of sight. Unless they scoped the place first, whoever came in wouldn't know that I was there, which was fine with me. I took the nine mil out from under my jacket, and waited.

A few minutes passed before the front door opened. The sound was soft and slow—somebody was being careful. I was hoping that they would be careful but not too careful. It would be nice to have someone alive to question. No more knee shots.

Soft footsteps moving in the hallway. As quietly as I could, I stepped out of hiding. It worked okay until I stepped on a broken light bulb.

A tan trench coat, a tan hat, and.. high heels.

"Take it slow, and turn around with your hands up in the air," I said. I might not be a detective, but I was sure getting to sound like one.

The blonde hair should have given her away. It was Vickie. I was going to lower the gun, but had second thoughts.

"What the hell are you doing here?" I asked.

"You first," she said.

She looked good in a trench coat, like one of those models in a television commercial for exotic lipsticks.

"I've got the gun, don't I?"

"Like you'd shoot me," she replied sarcastically.

She was right. It was a cheap line.

I put my gun back in its holster.

"Okay, truce," I said. "See, the gun's back where it should be."

"And what are you doing here?" she asked.

"Looking for clues," I said.

"Had a change of heart?"

"Sort of," I admitted. "It's been getting on my nerves, so I thought that I would see what I could do. You, too?"

She shook her head. Her hair whipped to one side and then back again. Quiet on the set.

"Then what's with the trench coat and the hat? Not that it doesn't look sharp on you."

"I like this outfit," she said pointedly.

I remembered my response when Billy had ragged on my coat.

"Okay, I said truce already. So why are you here?"

"I just came to check on the place," she said.

But she was lying. I have a lot of experience with liars. In my old line of work, before I got retired, you got that kind of exposure. Mrs. Alderton said that I was jaded. Like she wasn't.

"Water the flowers, that kind of thing?"

"Yes, if you must know. I have a right to be here. Davey asked me to look after the place before he left, same as he always did."

Her voice was a gentle finger caressing my throat; a warm and musky smell on a hot summer night. But I still didn't like her, and she was lying to me on top of that. It didn't make me happy. Back in those days, not much did. Least of all, Vickie Matisse.

"Do you know why he went to Toronto?" I asked her.

"Business," she replied.

"What kind of business?" I asked.

"I don't know, he never said. You know how Davey was."

"Yeah."

Always a deal or a scam going down. I knew how Davey was.

"Who did this?" she asked, waving her hand around the disaster.

"I don't know."

"Should we be here?" she asked nervously. "What if they come back?"

"They're all through here. I don't think that we have to worry about that. Besides, I don't think that they were really looking for anything; they were just trying to make it look as though they were. If they were really looking for something, this place wouldn't look like this. They won't be back."

I heard another car pull into the driveway. She looked at me and I shook my head.

"Maybe they forgot something?" I suggested.

"What do we do now?" she asked.

"Get your hat and coat off," I told her. "I hope you're wearing something distracting."

She pursed her lips and cocked her head to one side.

"Hurry," I urged.

"You want to use me as bait?" she asked.

"Hurry," I repeated.

She gave me a look that her father would have been proud of. She was, after all, a Matisse, which was another reason that I didn't like her. Anatolio Matisse had once been on the other side of an enforcement contract I had handled for Lydia. There were no problems, but it wasn't love at first sight between Nat and I.

He had been a small-time hood at the time, looking to make a mark; I was much worse back then. I was fresh out of Viet Nam, where I had killed more people in a month than Nat would kill in a lifetime. I was a bad piece of work back then; Nat was bad, but war was worse.

Nat Matisse wanted power that was his coin. He got it any way that he could; used anything that worked. Murder for hire, however, had been his stock in trade. He got off on it.

There was a story going around years back that illustrates the point. He had a contract from a drug family to eliminate a competitor. "You fix it," the Colombian had told him, "so that the bastard can't reproduce."

The man's name was Raphael Alvarado. He lived in Miami on a nice street in an expensive home. He had lawn flamingos out front, an Olympic pool out back. And a family. A wife named Candy and two sons. Nat killed Raphael, Candy, and the two kids. He took an extra long time with Candy. He raped and tortured her for four hours, and in the end, beat her to death. He was a little bit more merciful with the kids, whom he just shot in the head. Raphael died the hardest. Having a spike pounded up your ass is no way to go. But that's what Nat did before he hit the big time enough to pay other people to do it for him.

That's the story that was going around, anyway. But the bodies of Raphael, Candy, and their two kids were never found, so it's kind of tough to verify.

I would say that I digress, but I'm not sure what the word means. Anyway, back to his daughter sheathed in her provocative outfit.

"That'll do," I told Vickie.

She wore a tight white dress that ended about four inches below her crotch. No doubt about it, she was distracting.

"Now hurry down the hall and stand where they can see you when they open the door. Move."

"This better work," she said, and, after throwing her coat and hat on top of the mess in the living room, hustled down the hallway. It was something to watch.

Just as she made it to the kitchen, I heard the doorknob turn.

I took a deep breath and waited. The door opened, and swung inward on its hinges.

Come on in, I thought, *I've got a surprise for you.*

"Miss Matisse," I heard a familiar voice inquire, "is Mr. Sulu here? Miss Retkin would like to see him."

For the second time that day, I put my gun away.

"I'm in here, Alain," I said.

He rounded the corner and came into the living room with an air of drama hanging about his shoulders like a cloak. Alain Denis, Lydia Retkin's right hand man wasn't hired for his good looks, but it would be an easy mistake to make. Tall, wide shouldered, with a mane the color of lion's fur that hung to his shoulders—he was everything that women want a man to look like, if you believe what you see on the cover of romance magazines. He didn't do much for me.

"I'm sorry to interrupt you, Mr. Sulu," he said deferentially, "but the lady would like to meet with you."

"I'm busy," I said. "Can't you see that I'm looking for clues?"

Alain cast his icy gray eyes around the room, and then brought them back to me. "Now, Mr. Sulu. It's urgent."

Not much of a sense of humor for a guy who couldn't be over twenty-five years old. He took his own looks way too seriously. I had always suspected that he flexed in front of the mirror at home to music when nobody else was around.

Vickie came from down the hall to get her things without so much as a look at me. She gave Alain a serious once-over before putting on her coat and hat and heading out the front door.

"Men," was all she said on the way out.

"Women," I said to the door as she slammed it behind her.

Alain stared at me dispassionately, without saying a word.

"You know," I finally said, "if we could combine your looks and my personality, we could be irresistible to women."

"Miss Retkin is waiting," he said without a smile.

I don't do comedy well.

CHAPTER 3

❁

A wide-open riot of flowers exploding in noisy colors. I hated meeting Lydia in her garden. She had this enamel white wrought iron table with a glass top that she usually sat at like she was posing for a magazine photo op. A pink pastel umbrella on a long white pole that went through a hole in the center of the glass shaded her from the sun, what there was of it since a herd of bloated gray clouds had moved in and taken over half of the sky.

"Jason, how nice of you to come," she said, as though I really had a choice.

Alain walked over and stood behind her right shoulder to stand guard as though she were a queen, and he her royal bodyguard.

"It's good to see you again, Lydia," I said. "You look great."

"Yes, I know," she said.

And she did.

She wore a finely cut pale blue blouse that matched the color of her eyes and white slacks. No jewelry. Her lustrous black hair cut whimsically short, her face, and her aerodynamically contoured body were enough.

"You wanted to see me?" I asked, pulling back a wrought iron chair and sitting directly across from her. The metal tips of the chair made a raucous grating sound against the concrete as I settled in.

"Coffee, Jason?" she asked, nodding toward an insulated pitcher on the table and an empty cup.

"Thanks," I said, and poured myself a cup.

Seconds tipped away as I took a sip and she appraised me. I felt like a kid who's been called into the principal's office unexpectedly, not knowing if he's screwed up or has done something good, but can't remember which.

"I was sorry to hear about your friend Davey," she said.

I knew that Mrs. Alderton had to her. I didn't know why she had done so.

"Thanks," I said. I didn't tell her about wanting to kill himself. It was none of her business.

She stared at a point over my left shoulder and drummed the fingers of her right hand lightly on the glass tabletop. Alain stood behind her as still as a guard at Buckingham Palace.

"Davey," she finally said, her eyes still off in the distance, "was trying to involve himself in a bit of my business."

I waited for her to continue. There was no percentage in trying to interrupt Lydia Retkin.

"Were you aware of that?"

"No," I said. "Not at all."

"That's a shame," she said. "You know how I feel about people involving themselves in my business."

"What was his scam?"

"Nothing that you need be concerned about, Jason dear. Alain will look after it. You're retired, remember?"

"I keep reminding myself."

"But you look fit enough."

Alain permitted himself a slight smirk. So I was forty-five years old? So what?

"I try to keep in shape."

"Yes, well, it's been nice seeing you again, Jason. Try to keep in touch, will you? Perhaps we could have a drink sometime."

Perhaps hell would freeze over first.

"Sure. Anytime."

"That will be all," she said. "Thank you for coming."

I was being dismissed, and I didn't much like it. I was about to push back my chair, when I decided to take a wild shot.

"It wouldn't involve Traxor, would it?" I asked.

Suddenly her eyes were focused directly on my own. I had gotten the lady's attention. She stared at me hard, as though trying to read how much I knew. Behind her, Alain seemed to tense. Finally, she made up her mind.

"Don't be a stranger," she said.

Bluff called.

"You know I love you," I told her, "but I'm just not good enough for you."

"Humph," replied Mrs. Alderton.

Her gray hair was tied back in a pink and white tie-dyed scarf. As she dunked her tea bag up and down in her favorite cup, a souvenir of her pilgrimage to see The Phantom of the Opera in Toronto, she pursed her lips together tightly.

"We could get married," I continued, "but I don't want to embarrass you. You've got your reputation to consider, I know."

We were sitting in the kitchen, where I had first read on Sunday about Davey's death. The same kitchen where Mrs.A had killed the two intruders. I looked around. Everything was in order; everything was clean to the point of sparkling. In my experience a room never looks quite so good as after someone's been killed in it and professional Company cleaners have come in to make it spotless.

"What is it you want, Jason?"

"You're hurting my feelings, Mrs. A."

"Jason Sulu, you're never this sweet to me unless you want something. Now, what is it?"

I wanted to ask her why she had ratted on me to Lydia Retkin, but that would be pointless. She had an arrangement with Lydia, I knew that much. Looking after me was part of the deal. When I first found out that I had a sixty-three year old bodyguard, it didn't do much for my ego. I went a little ballistic on Lydia and Mrs. Alderton both, but I got over it the day that she shot Alvin Willowby between the eyes.

Alvin was a friend of Nat Matisse. Nat had sent Alvin and two of his associates to meet me on Belle Isle to discuss some outstanding business. I had been retired about a year, and really had no contact with Nat at the time. It was Vickie who passed the message through Davey to me. If it hadn't been through his daughter, I would have given it more serious thought. I thought that I was going to meet Nat. I didn't know that he was sending three of his goons.

I went unarmed. It was supposed to be that type of meeting. Of course, earlier in the day I had stashed a weapon under the park bench we were supposed to meet at, but that was standard procedure with me. I didn't expect to have to use it.

Mrs. Alderton was good; I never knew that she was shadowing me until she shot Alvin.

It was a hot night in August, it was dusk, the Belle Isle park had pretty well cleared out, and I was face to face with Alvin. His two friends were behind me. I should have known something was up when Alvin, who looks a lot like Nat from a distance, showed up in a sports coat. But I was already well into retirement mode by that time.

Alvin, like Vickie's father Nat, was about five foot five, with a full head of black, greasy hair, a big featured face with a flattened nose, and shoulders almost a third as wide as he was tall. When he spoke, however, his voice, was deeper, harsher, destroyed by a three pack a day habit.

"We're going to take a walk, you and me," he said.

"What's this all about, Alvin?" I asked.

I was standing at the bench that had the gun taped beneath it. If it weren't for the fact that there were two men behind me with guns, it would have been a different story, but as it was, I was getting no slack.

The park bench stood beside a jogging trail. A stainless steel drinking fountain was three feet away, but other than that; there was nothing for a thirty-foot radius around the bench. I was screwed.

"You and your friends been messing where you shouldn't have been messing," he said.

His legs were spread apart, his thumbs hooked in his pants' pockets. He'd seen, I remember thinking, too many gangster movies and listened to too many Nancy Sinatra songs.

My mind was on overdrive. I had been in a lot of tight spots in my life, but that one looked just plain hopeless. There was nothing that I could do—I had been brain stupid to go in the first place. If it hadn't been Vickie and Davey that had passed on the message, I wouldn't have gone. For some reason, I just wasn't going to let Vickie think that I was afraid of her old man.

"Alvin," I had said, "I don't have a clue what you're talking about. Can you give me a hint? I'm retired, you asshole."

"Retired? Really? Well, you could have fucking fooled me," he replied.

"What do I have to do to convince you?" I asked.

I was way nervous by that time. The thing was that there was really nothing that I could think of to do except to try and talk my way into an opening. Alvin and his friends weren't amateurs.

"To convince me? For starters," he replied, pulling a silenced pistol from inside his coat and beading the sites directly on where my heart would be if it didn't leap right out of my throat before he could pull the trigger, "for starters, you could die, peckerhead."

Right then was when his forehead exploded, spraying red blood, flesh, and bone fragments out the back of his skull. I dropped to all fours and scrambled for the pistol taped beneath the park bench, expecting a bullet in the back at any second from one of the two men who had been behind me.

I got my head underneath the bench and rolled over onto my back. My hand groped beneath the bench. I felt dried gum, something else that I couldn't and wasn't interested in identifying, and tape, peeled back and hanging down.

No gun.

I heard a man's voice say "son of a bitch", and glanced back toward where the men had been standing. One of them, the younger one with the blond hair, was down. The other had a pistol in his hand and one was fanning the environment, looking for someone to nail.

"Son of a bitch," I heard him say, "son of a fucking bitch."

His face was hard to see, the way he kept whipping his head around, but when he finally settled on me, I could see that he had made up his mind. He stopped fanning the park. If he was going down, I was, too.

I shoved the ground hard and scooted another body length past the bench, but it was no use. I closed my eyes.

Nothing.

No bullet.

I opened my eyes again in time to see him topple backwards and drop to the ground. Three men down in maybe thirty seconds, and nobody in sight. I held my breath and lay motionless.

Movement in the tree line.

A dark, slight figure moving across the grass toward me. She was maybe twenty feet away when I recognized her.

At first, I thought that she was going to do me, too. I never her told her that, then, or since. But I think she knew what I was thinking.

"You shouldn't lay in wet grass, Jason," she said, "you'll catch a cold."

"I'm comfortable," I told her. I wasn't about to show her how shook up I was. It was bad enough that she had to save my ass.

She was cradling a scoped rifle in her arms as though it were a baby. The park was silent, humid, and hot, like a lion's cage must be at night when the beast is sleeping.

"And you should find better friends," she told me, looking around at the three dead men.

"Yeah, well, I don't get out much to meet new people," I said from where I lay.

"I can see why," she said. "Come on, now, let's go home."

So we did. Things were different after that. I quit bitching to Lydia about her. And I never questioned what her arrangement with Lydia was regarding me after that incident.

Which was why that day in the kitchen I tried a different tack. She had let Lydia know about Davey, and that I was checking around. That was part of her job, to keep Lydia informed and to keep an eye one me when she thought I needed it. Maybe her job didn't include keeping me informed about Lydia, but maybe it didn't restrict her, either. I had to find out about Traxor and what it had to do with Davey's death.

"Mrs. A.," I said, "I'm always sweet to you."

"Uh-huh," she said, throwing her tea bag into the wastebasket.

She came and sat at the table, bringing her cup with her.

"What is it you want?" she asked when she had settled comfortably into her chair.

The magic moment.

"I want to know about Traxor," I told her, "and why it's so important that it got Davey killed, the company headquarters leveled in an explosion, and people bothering us. Can you tell me that?"

"Curiosity..." she began.

"I know," I said. "It got the cat killed. I don't want to be curious, Mrs. A., I want to know enough so that I don't go looking where I shouldn't. If I knew what was going on, I could avoid that. Can you help me?"

She considered the matter, took a sip of tea, and pursed her lips.

"No," she said at last.

"No?"

"No," she repeated.

"I don't want to get on Lydia's bad side…"

"Then let it go, Jason. You're retired, remember?"

Here's what I had always wondered—if I got out of line, would Mrs. A. take me out? Was that a part of her job, too? And if so, how would she do it? I didn't think that she'd shoot me, we had become too good of friends for that. Maybe cyanide in my coffee…

"I know, but Davey was my friend, and your gentlemen callers are getting a bit rough these days."

"Hmmm."

"I'm not complaining or anything, but I would like to know what's going on."

She took another sip of tea and gave me a grandmotherly look.

"I never ask questions, Jason," she said gently, "and neither should you."

"He was my friend."

I didn't mention the fact that I had planned on killing him after he had told me from his car phone how he had sat by and let my sister die.

"Was, dear boy, is the operative word. He's dead, now. You should concentrate on other things."

"Like what?" I asked irritably. "I'm retired, now. I've got nothing to do except rattle around in this museum of a house. What kind of a life is that for a man who still has a decent sperm count in his body?"

She smiled a little at that, and absently ran a hand across her still firm-looking breasts.

"Dead men," she advised me, "can't get it up."

Mrs. Alderton had a point.

"Not the headquarters," said Billy Bumper to me over the telephone, "the main R&D center. I never said it was their headquarters.

I don't make mistakes when it comes to information. I got my professional pride, you know."

I was standing in a phone booth at a gas station two miles from home. No reason to call from home. Anymore, I got the uncomfortable feeling that I didn't have an untapped line in the place.

"Okay, so it was the fucking R&D lab that was vaporized. What the hell kind of research did they do there, Billy?"

"Why are you asking me?" he asked. "It was in all of the papers. You don't need to pay me for this kind of chump change. Not that I'll refuse your money, you understand."

"Are you going to tell me or not? I'm getting tired of shoving quarters into this fucking phone."

I hadn't even used my calling card number to charge the call. That could be traced.

"Okay, okay. Artificial intelligence for computers. That kind of shit."

"Artificial intelligence?" I asked. What did that have to do with the price of the bullet that killed Davey?

"Big money stuff, tough guy. Computers that think. Heavy money in that kind of research."

Heavy money. Lydia would be interested in that. So would Davey. Years ago, I would have been, too.

"Please insert fifty cents," intoned the digitally created operator.

"Fuck you," I replied.

"Fifty cents," insisted the computer-generated woman.

"Bitch," I said as I inserted the money.

"You're losing it, man," said Billy.

"Could you be a little more specific?"

"Sure, I mean, like, you're talking to a machine, man," he replied.

"I mean about the artificial intelligence stuff," I said impatiently.

"Oh, you mean the AI? That's what they call it."

"Yeah, what you said."

"I'll have to do some digging. That'll cost you."

"Go figure," I said.

"I'll get back to you."

"No, Billy, I'll get back to you. I'm not taking calls at home anymore."

"Is this getting heavy?" he asked. "Because I'll have to up the price if t is."

"Just get it done, Billy. How much time do you need?"

"Two days," he said. "Maybe more."

"I'll call you in two days," I said, and then hung up.

The little prick was really starting to get on my nerves.

Vickie Matisse knew something. I didn't know what, or if what she knew would even help me out, but she knew something. I went to her apartment to try and find out what it was.

"You don't got no business with my daughter," Nat Matisse told me. "None. No business at all, you understand?"

I should have called first; then I would have known that her dick of a father might be there—and Marty and some another associate.

"Sure, Nat, I understand," I said.

What else can you say to a man who has two men pointing guns at you? But I shouldn't have called him Nat; in those days he liked to be called

Mr. Matisse.

"I don't think you understand nothing," he said suspiciously. "I think you've got shit for brains."

Nat never knew that it was Mrs. Alderton who had whacked his three men in the Belle Isle Park, and I had never told him. I wouldn't exactly say that Nat was afraid of me, but he didn't take any chances with me, either. With his two men pointing guns at me, however, he seemed to be considering getting me out of his hair permanently.

"Mr. Matisse," I said carefully, "I understand now that I should stay the hell away from your daughter. I was just coming here because she asked me to check in on her after Davey died, but I know now to keep a respectful distance, and I'll abide by that."

Nat ran a hand through his greasy black hair. He was an unpleasant man to look at, with thick, bushy eyebrows, a broken nose, and skin the color of a monkey's bare ass. I wondered again for the millionth time how a slug like Nat Matisse could have had a daughter as beautiful as Vickie. Then again, I had never met her mother.

Vickie was tucked away in her bedroom, following her father's instructions to get the hell out of the room. She had left the living room and gone dutifully into her bedroom, closing the door softly behind her. Daddy was still Daddy.

"A respectful distance? I like that," he said.

He would. I'd figured he'd watched the Godfather so many times that his VCR could play it without the tape even being in the machine.

"She's your daughter," I said.

Men like Matisse had unbelievably big egos. They jacked off on power.

"Damn right she is," he nodded.

"Then, if it's all right with you, I'll be on my way."

The trick was to play the scene out in from of his two men. I had to look and sound like I was asking permission. That made it better for Nat, whom I would damn well deal with later. At that moment, however, I needed to get out alive.

"Daddy?"

Vickie's door had opened and she was sticking her lovely face out at what I judged to be the worst possible moment.

"Get back in your room," ordered her father.

"No," she said.

"Get back in your room," he repeated, his voice getting quieter as he repeated the order.

"Daddy, I asked Jason to come here."

"I was just leaving," I told her.

"No—."

"Yes," I said, "Your father and I agreed that it was a mistake for me to come here in the first place."

"I don't care," Nat, told her, "if the Pope himself invited him. He doesn't belong here. You get out of here," he said to me, "and don't come back."

"Yes, sir," I said.

I tried not to look directly at Vickie, hoping that she would let it go, which she did. An hour later, I was in Wyandotte, a hick suburb about thirty minutes south of Detroit.

Anita's office was on the second floor of washed out white building on Biddle Avenue. The first floor was a bar/restaurant called Shylock's, where I used to hang out before I noticed that I was hanging out.

"TRAKM" was stenciled in black letters over the frosted white glass of her door window. I opened it without knocking. In the Downriver area, any customer is pretty much welcome since the auto industry started going straight down the shitter. Anita used to get a lot of competitive intelligence work from the Big Three before they started in-housing a lot of their on-line search work. She was discreet and she was good.

I saw her sitting where her secretary usually sat. Her hair was pulled back into a bun, she wore horned rimmed glasses with lenses so thick that her eyes looked a fourth again larger, and she wore a dark, properly prim dress that did nothing for her figure. At only thirty-three years old, she looked well on her way to being a black belt old maid. But when she took off her glasses, let down her hair, and sleazed up a bit, she was a whole different woman. I can say that from experience.

"Hey, Anita," I said. "Wake up."

"Just a minute," she replied without looking up from her computer screen.

"Where's Julie?" I asked.

"Just a minute," she repeated, punching a rapid-fire set of keystrokes that sounded like a line of Black Cat firecrackers popping.

"Anita Allison," I said, "your message has been received."

I closed the door behind me softly, and took a seat in one of the chairs against the wall. Magazines that I wouldn't read were stacked on a short wooden coffee table in front of me. After a moment she looked up and started, as though surprised to see me sitting there.

"Good morning," I said.

Confused, she looked at her watch.

"It's afternoon," she scolded.

"Yeah, but you're just waking up," I said.

Anita and I had had a thing going on a ways back, but that was definitely past history. The sex was great, but the inside of her head was wired wrong. She should wear a T-shirt that would read "Dangerous when Wet."

"Would you leave me alone?" she snapped. "I've had a hell of a day."

"Sorry," I said.

She stretched her arms back and over her head, a neat trick that I remembered well from other circumstances.

"Now," she said, when she had concluded her stretch, "what is it that you want?"

"Some help."

"It'll cost," she said.

"I can remember when it didn't."

"Your loss, cowboy."

"Yeah," I agreed, and I half meant it.

"You want some coffee?"

"No, thanks. I'm wired already."

"Then tell Anita. What is it that you want?"

"I want some dirt on a company called Traxor. They're Canadian. And I don't want the database shit. I want real dirt—on their artificial intelligence division. Something going on up there got a friend of mine killed. You heard about Davey, right?"

She shook her head no, so I told her what I knew. Usually, Anita doesn't like extraneous information when she's doing a job for me, but I figured she should know about Davey before getting involved.

"I'm sorry, Jason," she said.

"Yeah, thanks. Something else you should know," I said, steeling myself for her reaction. "I got Bumper on this job, too."

"You're an asshole," she said, her lips pulling back the way that vampires do before they bite.

"Yeah, thanks."

"I mean it."

"I know, and you're right. But it's for Davey."

"I don't know if I want the job," she said.

"Oh, you want the job, Anita. Whoever finds what I need first, gets their tab doubled."

She considered that for a moment.

"How much of a head start did you give him?" she finally asked.

"Nothing," I said. "All right, maybe a day."

"A day? You gave him a day? How is Anita supposed to catch up?"

I hated, almost more than anything else about her, her tendency to talk about herself in the third person. It gave me a headache.

"I'll give you what he's given me already."

She was out of her chair and around her desk. I know it's a cliché, but she really was as fluid as a cat. Her purple dress hung mid-calf, but clung to her as she stepped toward me. The dress buttoned up the front, and I noticed that it pulled tightly in the chest area. I tried to console myself with the fact that I had seen her breasts before, that they were lined with unattractive stretch marks, and that I'd had them before anyway. She stopped a foot away from me.

"Anita's hungry, Jason. Why don't you take her downstairs and feed her?"

"Love to," I said, "but I've got to get a move on."

I waited for her to back up so that I could get up without crushing up against her.

"You've got to get a hard on?" with a sly wink.

"A move on. Places to go, killers to catch."

"Ohhhh...."

"Yeah, well, there it is. Sorry. Help me out, though, will you? Find me something that will help me catch up to Davey's killers."

When I finally escaped her office, I felt the way that I always do—that maybe I shouldn't have come in the first place.

CHAPTER 4

"It's called 'Dead Wait,'" she explained.

"What?" I asked.

Dr. Marianne Corey was a lead that Anita provided me with by the next morning. She sat in front of her computer downloading, as she had explained, some files for some invisible location on the Internet. The wait was annoying, but I had to patient. I had finally had a lead into Traxor. Maybe she would turn out to be a suspect. I just knew that my decoder ring was in the mail already.

"The lag time," she said, the annoyance in her voice making it clear that my presence irritated her as much as hers irritated me. "You know," she continued, "while the information is downloading."

"Why?"

With a quick flick of her head, she tossed her mess of red hair back over her shoulders, and tilted her head to one side. The flickering of the screen repeated itself in the lenses of her glasses. Red hair and green eyes were my favorite combination, but she had too plain of a face for me to find her attractive. Her lips were full enough, bone structure was great, and she had something of a body beneath her lab coat, but it didn't make up for her plain Jane look. Maybe she worked at it, I couldn't tell, but a little make-up wouldn't have hurt her. I'm not into geishas or anything, but I like the drama in a woman's face that comes from blush or rouge or whatever it is that they apply to give depth and color to their faces.

"Named after the late Arnold Lampl," she said without looking up.

"Is that right…"

"Right as rain, Mr. Sulu. Anybody ever ask you to beam them up?"

"Scotty. It was Scotty. Remember? 'Beam me up, Scotty.' That's the way that it went."

"You must have been alive when that show first started on TV," she said, looking up and showing me a quick smile that disappeared almost as soon as it appeared. "Anyway. Arnold Lampl was a computer scientist of little note except for one thing."

"And that was?"

"He died of a heart attack sitting in front of his terminal waiting for information to download. He had a 300 bps modem. That's why they call the download time Dead Wait."

"Lovely," I said.

"You have to understand technical humor."

"Right."

"Look, Mr. Sulu, I've got a lot of work to do, so maybe you could tell me exactly what it is that you want to know."

That was the problem; I didn't know exactly what to ask. I wasn't totally computer illiterate, but artificial intelligence was a little over my head. "Well?" she pressed.

Well…

"Is the name David Wiltz familiar to you?"

"Should it be?" she countered.

"Never heard of him, then?"

"Could you perhaps give me a clue as to what it is that you want?"

"I was hoping that's what you would give me," I said.

"Mr. Sulu," she said, "I'm not sure what it is that you want."

"A friend of mine was killed," I said, trying a different tack. "His name was David Wiltz. "I'm beginning to think that it had something to do with computers."

"I'm sorry to hear that your friend died," she said, "but I'm not familiar with his name, and 'something to do with computers' is a little too vague for me to be of much help to you. I don't know what else to tell you." "You could tell me something about the seamy side of computing, for a start."

With an automaton-like movement, she swiveled her chair to face mine directly. At the lower edge of my vision, I could see that the hem of her skirt, even sitting down, hung two inches below her knee.

"What are you talking about?" she asked, as though talking to an aberrant child.

"Seamy, as in crooked; that sort of thing."

"Mr. Sulu," she said as she smoothed her lap, "my field is artificial intelligence. It took me twelve long years of schooling and work to get me to where I am today. Artificial intelligence has no seamy side; there is nothing crooked about it."

There was a slight flush developing in her cheeks as she took a deep breath before continuing.

"Do you know why I got into computers in the first place, Mr. Sulu?"

I didn't bother to answer, but shrugged my shoulders instead. It wasn't like she gave a shit what I said or thought anyway. I wasn't in her league. I didn't carry a personalized pocket protector.

"Well, I'll tell you," she continued, as though I had asked. "Because I don't like to be around people like you."

It was a little harder line than I had expected I have to admit.

"I don't like vague questions, snide implications, or people too weak minded or poorly prepared to conduct clearly thought out inquiries."

"Pardon?" I asked. "I'm just trying to get a clue, lady, a place to start. This guy was my friend, and I'd like to at least get an idea of why he died. Cut me some slack here, will you?"

"Then why," she demanded, "are you talking to me? I didn't know your friend, and I don't know what you want. What kind of detective are you, anyway?"

"I'm not a detective." She was beginning to piss me off. She talked to me like I was a student that she was reprimanding.

"Then what are you?"

"I'm a friend of the man who died."

"And why are you talking to me instead of the police?"

Bullshitting her was obviously out of the question.

"Because you're doing research on artificial intelligence for Traxor, and whatever got Davey killed had something to do with AI."

"How did you know that I did work for Traxor?"

She was about ready to seriously ramp up on me again.

"Don't go paranoid on me," I told her. "I read about it."

She stood to her full height. She must have been six two or three, even in her flats, but she looked a lot taller from where I sat.

"It wasn't in the papers," she said in a flat, cold voice.

Oops.

"I didn't mention the newspapers," I said evenly.

She blinked, but stayed on course. "Then where did you read about it?"

"I'm getting tired of being interrogated," I told her. I could have stood up to level the body language playing field, but it wouldn't have gotten me

Anywhere. She would still have been an inch or two or, sure, maybe even four taller.

"Then leave," she said, extending her right hand toward the door.

"Okay."

I stood up, and started walking toward the door. She didn't say anything to stop me, so when I got my hand wrapped around the door knob, I turned to her and asked, "Hey, Doc, how much money could I get if I stole the guts of your work and hawked it to the competition?"

Her mouth dropped open only a quarter of an inch, but from where I stood, it would have liked to have dropped another two.

I didn't wait for her to reply, but turned and left without closing the door behind me.

As fact-finding missions went, my meeting with Dr. Corey hadn't gotten much in the way of results. I had learned, however, that when it came to AI, unless you were a member of the fraternity—or sorority—you were SOL when it came to getting them to open up.

Anita had phoned me the lead the next morning after our meeting, telling me that Dr. Corey was sleeping, rumor had it, with the headman for AI research at Traxor, whose name was Lawrence Meshke, Ph.D., who probably did not go by the nickname of Larry. It was Lawrence Meshke who had been on the phone with Dr. Roper when Davey was patched into their conversation.

What had begun to bother me was that, although I have had the experience of using a portable phone and, in the middle of talking to one person, ending up talking to someone else, they had never been able to hear me. I could hear both ends of their conversation, but they could never hear me, no matter how much I yelled. That being my experience, I wondered how it was that they could have become aware that Davey was privy to their conversation. If they were not aware that Davey had listened in, where was the connection between the crossover of calls and Davey's death? If there were no linkage there, then why would they come after me?

Marianne Corey was the closest thing that I had to an inside lead, and I would have to talk with her again. On the front end, I had just wanted to stir her up a bit, to make her nervous. After meeting her, however, I suspected that she wasn't the nervous type. The next time that I visited her, however, I would need some stronger ammunition if I hoped to break loose any information from her.

From Marianne's AI laboratory, I headed back home, taking the long and depressing route down Fort Street. I avoid I-75 like the plague as a matter of habit, and have ever since I moved to Detroit. If you drive through Detroit, you could be going through just any seedy city in America. To really get the feel of the burned out shell that Detroit is, you need to stick to the regular roads.

It's not that Detroit has more vacant buildings than any of the other big cities, but it sure as hell is a lot emptier. When the white flight thing hit Detroit, it was pretty much a matter of knock-knock, nobody home from then on. The city won't feel populated again until the folks that left or their children have the balls to move back. Meantime, I like to drive around and feel the emptiness. Mrs. Alderton says that it's a Freudian reinforcement—kind of like taking a bus tour of my own soul. She half-smiles when she says it, but, unless I'm imagining it, her eyes were an icier blue when we discussed it.

Mrs. A. was out by the time that I arrived home. My house, I realized, felt as empty as the city in which I lived. Then again, maybe I was being overly Freudian.

I went straight to my study, hung my coat on the back of the door, and collapsed into the burgundy leather chair behind my desk. The back of my head rested on the top of the chair, but still I wasn't comfortable enough so I rolled the chair back a little and swung my feet up onto the corner of the desk. The house was silent, save for the soft electrical hum of my computer, which, when I closed my eyes, sounded a little like the noise that fluorescent lights make when you're close enough to hear them.

Davey, Davey, I thought, who did you piss off?

After a while, I began to feel guilty doing nothing, although I had done a lot of that for the last few years, and decided to check my computer for calls. With my feet still resting on the corner of the desk, I leaned forward, and flicked the monitor switch to "on." A graphical representation of an answering machine popped onto the screen.

I moved the cursor over to the message button and yawned.

"You have seven messages," said an automated voice remarkably similar to the one that I had heard from the phone company while talking to Billy Bumper. Press one to hear your messages. Press two to identify the callers. Press three to—."

I used the cursor-finger to press one as quickly as I could. There was no reason on God's green earth that I could think of to listen to options three through thirty.

The first caller was a hang up.

The second caller was a hang up.

The third caller was a hang up.

The fourth caller was a hang up.

The fifth caller was a weird mix of electronic squealing.

The sixth caller was the same screeching electronic mess and then I heard a single word. "Spider."

The seventh caller was the digital cat fight again, and then the words, "in the web."

"Well," I told the desk lamp, "that was something special. I was wondering where the spider was. The spider's in the web. The farmer's probably still hanging out in the dell, too."

My desk lamp, as usual, had no opinion.

Spider in the web, I mused. A clue? Not too damn likely, I decided. A threat? Maybe.

Something to do… that was my problem. I needed something to do other than talking to people and taking weird phone messages. I would feel a lot more productive if I could point a gun at somebody.

Spider in the web.

What did it mean? What was the caller trying to say?

The voice had been one of those electronic compendiums of twenty or thirty electronic voices blended together, so there was really no chance of identifying the caller, even with Billy Bumper's considerable computer resources. Still, it was worth a shot.

I took a diskette out from a desk drawer and inserted it into my "A" drive, and went to the answering machine programs "copy" function. Using the cursor, I identified the message file and the drive that I wanted to send it to, and clicked on the "OK" button.

After a moment's electronic thinking, the following message appeared on my screen:

Enter password

I had never seen that screen appear before when copying a voice file. I thought about that for a minute or two, and then typed in "logic1", which was my password. To my surprise, another message appeared on my screen. It said:

For your own protection, please type the following paragraph:

The first paragraph of the Gettysburg Address followed.

"What the shit?" I said to myself.

Instinctively, I rolled the chair back, stood up and drew my gun. I fanned the room like they do in the movies, and after a few moments, began to feel unaccountably stupid. If someone had gotten into the house and accessed my computer, that would mean that they had to get past the security system first, and if they had done that, then there was no point in drawing my gun. If they meant me harm, I would have already been dead—long dead. They could have activated an explosion the moment I got into the house; there was no reason to play games with me.

I holstered the nine mil again and sat down.

My security had been compromised. I was getting older, and I was definitely out of practice, but my security system was not older—it was state of the art. And it had been compromised. Somebody had had to be very, very good to do that.

I shot out of the chair again when it finally occurred to me that whoever it was might have taken out Mrs. Alderton. If they had killed her, then... then they were really good. The chances, however, were that she had gone to the store for a few minutes, so, with my gun in one hand, I took the phone off of the hook with the other, and punched in the number of her cellular phone. She answered it on the second ring.

"Mrs. A?" I asked before she could finish the word "hello."

"Jason?" she asked back.

"Right," I said. "Where are you at?"

"Why, dear? You sound out of breath."

She sounded okay, but she would under any circumstances. Mrs. Alderton was tough to upset. The good news was that she hadn't said any of the cryptic words that would alert me to trouble. The bad news was that she didn't know anything yet that could be of help.

"Just from working on my computer."

That would put her on alert. She knew that I didn't know anything about computers. My idea of fixing a computer was to shoot the damn thing and go buy another one.

"I see. And how is it going?"

"I need a little help on this one, Mrs. A. Would you mind coming back when you can—it doesn't have to be right this second—to see what you can do about it?"

"I've got another hour or so of shopping left, Jason," she said, "and I was planning on stopping at the bookstore before coming home. Can it wait until then?"

"No problem," I replied. "Get here when you can. I'll muddle through and try to get it fixed before you get home."

"All right, dear. Put some coffee on for me."

"Yes, ma'am," I said, and hung up.

Help was on the way.

The computer emitted a beep, and I glanced down at the screen. The words

Don't be afraid.

appeared and stayed on the screen for a few minutes, then disappeared to be replaced with the prior message instructing me to type in the first paragraph of the Gettysburg address. The actual paragraph that I was supposed to type was included, since whoever had sent the message in the first place had correctly assumed that I didn't know the first paragraph of the Gettysburg Address.

You're fucking with the wrong guy, asshole, I thought, although I had to admit that for the moment, whoever it was had the edge.

My eyes scanned the room, looking for something that wasn't as it should be. The door looked okay, the floor looked vaguely familiar, and the desk looked just as rectangular as the last time I had seen it.

Hurry up, Mrs. A., I thought.

It occurred to me at that moment that it could have been an inside job. Mrs. Alderton knew how to bypass the house security system. With Lydia Retkin involved, I wasn't sure which side of the fence that old lady was on. I knew that Mrs. Alderton cared a great deal for me, but she was a professional's professional. There was no way to ever be sure exactly what was on her mind, so I gave up trying. She would let me know when she was ready. All that I could do in the meantime was hope that she was on my side, and not try to do anything that would turn her against me.

You see, although I knew that Mrs. A. was contracted by Lydia Retkin to keep an eye on me, I knew that the old lady did not solely report to Lydia, nor was she solely responsible to her. Mrs. Alderton still had active links somewhere in the shadows of the U.S. government, and I was betting that neither Lydia Retkin nor myself ranked above whoever was really pulling the old babe's strings.

For the first time since I had gotten involved with tracking down whoever was responsible for Davey's death, I began to wonder if Mrs. Alderton's masters had an interest in Traxor and whatever was going on there. It was not a happy thought. Maybe that was why Mrs. A. was advising me to keep my nose out of it.

I was getting to the point that I knew that, from a tactical view, I should in fact lay low, but Davey Wiltz' had either killed my sister or not, and I needed to know which of the two options were real. If I found out that he had killed my sister, then the worms could eat him. But if he hadn't, then I owed it to him to even the score. Vickie Matisse had been right about that. As cold a person as she seemed to be, she did have a point.

In fact, I realized, the person most likely to know what had happened between Susan and Davey was probably Vickie. As emotional as Davey was, he would have needed to talk to someone, and he had probably talked to her. The question was, would she tell me? I could lean on her, but then I would have to deal with Nat and his boys. There would be no avoiding that, since, aside from the fact that she was his daughter, he had given me explicit instructions to stay the hell away from her.

"Jason?"

It was Mrs. Alderton, standing in the doorway, her Beretta aimed at my head. My stomach tightened as though it had been placed in a vice. She was dressed in blue slacks and a crème colored sweater that she had knitted herself. I know, I had seen her do it.

"I didn't hear you come in," I said.

My own gun was in my left hand, lying on the desk. She had a clean shot at me, and she never, ever missed. My stomach wasn't feeling any better. If she wanted me dead, I was about to be just that.

She lowered her gun.

"What's the problem?" she asked.

When Mrs. Alderton was on alert status, her lips looked thinner.

"Take a look," I said, motioning my head at the computer monitor. I released my hold on my Beretta and let it lay where it was.

"Do I need this?" she asked, inclining her head toward her gun.

"I don't have a clue," I shrugged. "You look at the screen and tell me."

When she hesitated, I reached over, grabbed the monitor with both hands, and swung it around so that she could see what was written there.

Mrs. A. frowned, deepening the wrinkles in her forehead. A frowning old person is not a nice thing to see. She drew in a soft breath through her nose, and then exhaled more loudly through her mouth.

"Do it," she said.

I reached for my gun.

"Not that, you ninny," she snapped. "Do what it says. Type in what it says."

"I need to look at the screen," I said. "I don't know the—."

"Just do it," she said.

"I was worried about the keyboard," I told her.

"Don't be," she said. "Trust me."

"Do you know something about this?" I asked her.

"I know that if you don't do what it says, we might be sorry that you didn't."

"You know that somebody has screwed with my computer," I said, "and anything could happen when I type in what it's asking for me."

"Get out of the chair, Jason, I'll do it."

"Mind if I stand out in the hall in case it blows up when you start typing?" I asked as I got out of the chair.

"Asshole," she replied.

"I've just got a bad feeling about this, that's all."

"So do I," she said. "Now move before I have to shoot you and drag your well-muscled body out of the way."

"Right," I said, and got the hell out of the way.

I noticed that her fingers hesitated a fraction of a second before typing.

I was standing over her left shoulder, and could see it plain as day.

She had typed maybe three or four lines, before the entire message disappeared, and a new one appeared. It said:

You are not Jason Sulu.
You will die.

"Uh-oh," I said.

"Shelter," Mrs. Alderton screamed.

I ran to the bookshelf, threw a handful of books aside and pressed the wooden panel behind where the books had been as hard as I could. The entire section began to swing away from the wall in what seemed to be slow motion. I noticed Tom Sawyer, Crime and Punishment, and a few other time-wasters before Mrs. Alderton yanked on my sleeve and pulled me around the corner and into the room behind. As we stepped into the metal room, I slapped a pressure switch on the wall and the bookshelf began to swing back into place. Mrs. Alderton pulled a wall lever at the back of the room, and I felt the hydraulics shift before the door closed and the room began to descend.

A soft electric light suffused the room with a yellowish glow, and I could see that Mrs. Alderton's face was grim.

"Son of a bitch," she muttered.

We were almost to the lower level when we felt, more than heard, the explosion rock the house.

CHAPTER 5

The newspapers headlined it as a gas explosion, which was kind of ironic since the now deceased Young Bob had showed up to kill me claiming that we had had a gas leak in order to get in the door. Of course, Young Bob was long past irony.

Billy Bumper took it harder than I did. We were having lunch—yes, again—at a seafood restaurant in Dearborn so that he could fill me in with what he had come up on, but I was having a hard time getting him off of the explosion.

The way that I look at near-death experiences is that when they're over, if you're still standing and have most of your body parts, there's no sense in dwelling on anything else except catching up with the people that tried to kill you.

Mrs. Alderton handled most of the interface with the cops, the government, and the newspapers, so that I was spared the agony of telling the same story over and over again. My opinion is that dealing with cops is usually worse than nearly getting killed. Dealing with reporters was worse than dealing with cops.

"What was it like?" he asked me for the fortieth time.

"It was loud, okay?"

"That's what you said last time," he said sullenly.

"Look, what more do you want me to say? It was just a bomb, Billy. It leveled the house, but it pissed me off more than anything. I didn't get a scratch on me, though. I can't see why you get so hung up on this kind of crap. It's not like I lost any body parts or anything."

"This is serious shit, Jason. I'm getting nervous."

"I hadn't noticed."

I would say he was nervous. By the time that we were halfway through the meal, he had stabbed himself twice in the cheek with his own fork, missing his mouth in one case by more than an inch.

"I got some stuff for you," he said. "But you're going to need to go to Toronto to check it out."

"I don't like Canada, Billy. It's too damn clean, and their money isn't worth shit."

"Very funny."

Billy was originally from Canada, some place called Sudbury that was big in steel and such. It was in the middle of nowhere to hear Billy talk about it, which he seldom did. I think he left in kind of a hurry.

"Yeah. So what have you got"?

The lobster shell that he had been picking over was pretty much gutted, and Billy wiped the butter from his chin with his napkin—serviette in Candianese—and reached inside of his checked polyester sports coat to pull out a sheaf of folded papers. Whatever Billy did with the money that I gave him, I was sure that he didn't spend it on clothes.

Billy's eyes darted around the restaurant, looking to see if anyone was interested. He reminded me of a kid looking around for to see if the convenience store manager was looking before he swiped some candy. He had been looking around every ten minutes or so, looking for any signs that any of the thirty or so other customers were a little too interested in us. "Give it a rest, Billy," I counseled him. "If you do things out in the open, and do them naturally, you got less chance of getting an ulcer."

I didn't believe it for a minute, but I wanted him to calm down. Reluctantly, he handed me the papers.

"Billy," I said before looking at the papers, "I've got to talk to you about something; it's about the bomb."

I hadn't planned on grilling him just yet, but I decided to bring it up anyway. Mrs. Alderton wouldn't like it if she found out, but that was just too bad. She had her way of doing things, and I had mine. I had to go with my guts.

"I thought that you didn't want to talk about the bomb anymore," he said, narrowing his eyes.

"This is different. I want to ask you about my computer."

While he listened, I filled him in on what had happened with my computer. I watched his face carefully while I talked, looking for any sign of guilt.

"How'd they get past your security?" he asked when I was finished.

"I don't know that they did, Billy. I've been thinking about it a lot, and maybe they didn't have to."

"Then how did they plant the bomb?"

I wasn't about to share my suspicions concerning Mrs. Alderton with him. Besides, it wasn't necessary. I was going to take him in another direction.

"Maybe the bomb was already in the house," I said. "Maybe it had been there for a long time."

"You mean somebody put a bomb in your house and you didn't even know it?"

"That's what I'm thinking."

"But," he protested, "don't you have the place swept for that? You're not exactly a popular guy with Nat Matisse and a few others. I just figured that you took precautions."

"I do. But if what I'm thinking is correct, I can understand why my people didn't catch it."

"What are you saying?" he asked.

"It's what I'm wondering that's important. I'm wondering whether or not the explosive could have been in my computer for a long time, just waiting to be triggered."

"No way," he said. "I built that computer for you myself."

"Yeah," I said, "I know that."

His face froze, as though it were made of sculpted ice. He must have sat there for a full minute before saying anything.

"You're not saying that you think that I did it?" he asked.

I didn't respond.

"You're an asshole, Jason. I can't believe that you'd turn on me."

I kept my expression neutral, then looked down at the papers in my hand.

"Fuck you," he said.

"What I can't figure out," I said without looking up, "is the password crap. If someone were trying to kill me, why would it go off after it had figured out that it wasn't me at the keyboard? And that's another thing, how did the computer know that it wasn't me sitting there?"

"So you don't think that I did it?"

"Billy, if I thought you did it," I said, raising my eyes to look directly into his own, "you wouldn't live through the salad, much less the lobster."

The truth was that I just didn't know what to think. In my experience, people will do most anything that they think they have to, circumstances permitting. Maybe Billy needed money a lot more than I knew, or maybe not. I made a mental note to have Anita check him out. While I was at it, maybe I'd have Billy check out Anita. It was too bad that I ever followed up on it.

"Thanks, I guess," he muttered.

"But I need your help on a couple of points. Let's forget the bomb for a minute, again. For now, tell me whether or not somebody could have access gotten the feeling that the real reason Billy hung with me was because he thought that someday, sometime, he would need me to keep him alive. William Bumper the Third seemed to have someone or something in his past that he was hiding from.

"What would something look like that could do that kind of damage?" he asked.

"I'm asking how they could have accessed my computer, not how they got a bomb in it, Billy. I'm not really sure where the explosive device was." "I know, but—."

"No buts. Could someone have accessed my machine through its modem connection or by some type of electromagnetic assault?"

"No way."

"You're sure?"

"No," he admitted, shaking his head.

"I'm thinking," I said, "of something like they use to control model airplanes, fine tuned to hook into my computer."

"It just isn't practical."

"How about something more mundane, like through the phone line that was connected to the computer?"

"Uh-huh. You're phone number isn't even on the books. I set it up myself. Even the phone company doesn't know it exists. How would anyone else even know what number to dial into?"

"For enough money, Billy, anybody can find out anything."

"Are you saying that I sold the phone number to your computer to somebody?"

His forehead was slightly flushed, and his cheeks were a shade brighter still than his forehead.

"No. All I'm saying is that if someone wanted me badly enough, and put enough people, enough money, and enough time into finding out how to get to me, that they could probably find that number."

"They'd have to have an awful lot of computer horsepower," he said.

"So?"

"Like a supercomputer."

"With enough money, someone could buy one. You get my point?"

Billy was starting to look genuinely worried.

"If they found out about your number, they might find out about me, too," he said, under his breath.

"I think you're starting to get the picture."

"This is bad," he said.

"Real bad," I said.

"I hate you," he said.

"Me too," I agreed.

"Hey, I just thought of something. Did you ever think of the fact that it blew because it wasn't you at the keyboard?"

"So?"

"Well, think about it this way—what would have happened if it was you at the keyboard?"

"Wipe your mouth, Billy; you missed some butter. And how the hell would my computer know who was at the keyboard."

Absently, Billy wiped his chin. "That could be done. Typing rhythms, for example. If someone had a profile of your typing rhythms, they could identify an impostor by matching the typing pattern to what was your established pattern in the database. And I wonder if it would have blown if it had been you doing the typing."

It was worth thinking about, but not much. Who in the hell would have a database that included my typing patterns? And why?

Mrs. Alderton had arranged temporary quarters for us at the Ritz Carlton in Dearborn. She suggested that we check in as husband and wife and share a room. I declined. I didn't have the heart to tell her that we could have checked in as mother and son. Besides, I didn't want to piss her off. She had room 304, and I had the adjoining room 302. There was a locked door between the two rooms, but it wasn't like a hotel room lock would stop her.

I had expected that Mrs. A. would have arranged a safe house for us. When she didn't, I registered the fact, but didn't question her. The explosion could have taken Mrs. Alderton out as well as myself. That fact had occurred to me some time after the incident. It had also occurred to me that for at least one set of enemies, Mrs. Alderton and I were on the same side.

After leaving Billy, I had planned to check in on the old lady, to see if there was something that she had found out that I could use, but I changed my mind at the last minute, and changed course to head toward Vickie Matisse' apartment.

Since I had had one of Billy's friends check my cellular phone for taps after the explosion, I felt safe enough to call her in advance.

"Vickie?" I said, when she was on the line.

"Jason?"

"Right. Are you okay to talk?"

"My father's not here, if that's what you mean," she said woodenly.

"That's what I meant. Could you meet me someplace?"

"Where?" she asked.

"How about Good Time Charlie's?" I asked.

"Where?" she asked again.

"Sorry, hang in there."

I thought that I must have been driving through a bad cell area. The phone had gone squirrelly for a moment, and she probably couldn't hear me. The brief white noise caused me to remember the night before Davey had died, when he had called me from his car phone. It nagged at me again that Billy had told me that Davey had been switched to another call in progress at Traxor. It had to have been arranged by someone. Why was something that I was completely in the dark about?

When the static had cleared, I repeated the name of the restaurant and hung up after I knew that she had it straight. I was about ten minutes from the restaurant when the car phone trilled.

"Sulu," I said, after punching it to hands-free status.

"Mr. Sulu," responded a familiar feminine voice. "This is Marianne Corey."

"Dr. Corey," I said. "I didn't expect to hear from you anytime soon."

"I didn't expect to be calling you, either."

"Then why are you calling?"

"I have gone through my records, and I have found no notes whatsoever for having met with a Mr. David Wiltz."

"You called me about that?" I asked.

"Not exactly," she replied, after waiting so long that I thought that we had lost our connection.

"Then why?"

"Could your friend have had an associate?"

I chewed on that what a moment before answering.

"Why do you ask?"

"Because," she said, "you are the second disagreeable man that I have spoken to in the last month. The first was a Mr. Danny Walker. Since Mr. Walker seemed to be rather… out of his element and not exactly on the up and up, I thought that he might be a partner of either yourself or your late friend."

It was quite a complement, in an offhanded way, and I was glad that she had made the connection. Danny Walker was one of Davey's many "working" names. But I wanted to be sure.

"Was Mr. Walker a very fat man, Dr. Corey?"

"He was considerably obese, Mr. Sulu. I dislike the term fat."

"Call it what you want, doctor. I call it fat."

"I should have known that you would prefer such a denigratory term."

"So are you going to tell me what the two of you talked about?"

"I would prefer to meet in person," she said.

"How about if I drive over to your lab after I finish up a meeting that I'm on my way to?"

"Perhaps," she said, "if it's not too much of an inconvenience to you schedule, we could meet for dinner instead. I'd prefer to discuss this elsewhere than on university grounds."

I was getting tired of meeting people for breakfast, lunch, and dinner, but I didn't want to pass up the chance for new information, so I agreed to meet her at six o'clock. Lunch shortly with Vickie Matisse, then dinner with Dr. Corey. It seemed like I was accomplishing more eating than investigating. I resolved to do a hundred extra sit-ups before going to bed that night.

Vickie Matisse was already waiting in a booth that was as far away from other diners as she could get. She was wearing faded blue jeans, a black turtleneck, and a herringbone sports coat. On anyone else, it might have looked bad, but on her, it looked attractive. Her outfit made her look like a college student. Women like her, I had long ago concluded, looked good in about anything.

Good Time Charlie's was a clone bar. It had the same brass banisters, the same framed newspaper clippings from the nineteen twenties, the same leaded glass hanging lamps that you see in every middle class food and drink establishment. It was like there was a factory somewhere that churned them out.

"Thanks for coming," I told her as I sat down.

The unintended sexual innuendo was lost on her, or maybe she just didn't care to acknowledge it. It was hard not to think about sex when I looked at her, just like it was hard not to think about death when I looked at her father. They were just natural reactions, so I wasn't too worried about my psychological stability.

"I'm sorry about my father," she said, absently flicking her hair away from her face.

"He can't help it," I said. "He's an asshole."

"He's a businessman," she said.

"Uh-huh," I replied.

"It's bad enough having him for a father, Jason, without having to endure your sarcasm. He's made some changes in his life; others will take more time. Right now, he's trying his hand at legitimate business. It isn't easy on him, and I'm not making excuses. I know what my father is and isn't."

"Well, he isn't a businessman, for starters," I said. "But tell me, how long has he been with computers and such?"

She shrugged, and I noticed her breasts move beneath her sweater. Five years ago, I would have noticed, but wouldn't have cared. On that day, however, I noticed and I noticed and I noticed.

"I thought you knew about his dealings with the Retkin people," she said.

Once again, the waiter's arrival, this time delivering potato skins, saved my mouth from dropping open in amazement.

"Are you trying to tell me that you're father's in the computer business with Lydia Retkin?"

"For someone who used to be in the know, Jason, you seem totally out of touch these days."

She was right. I felt like a man who gets up to turn off his television and notices for the first time that the walls and ceilings of his home have vanished sometime during the evening news.

"I think that you know that I was out of the loop, and I also think you know a lot more about everything than you're telling me," I said. "I know you've never liked me, Vickie, but do you have to get your kicks out of watching me stumble around like I'm blind?

"I don't get it. First you want me to find out who killed Davey, and then you don't tell me squat. Are we on the same team, or not? Or do you already know who killed Davey, and why they did it, and you're just waiting for me to catch up?"

"Poor Jason," she said. "You don't understand me at all, do you? You can't get by my looks to know me, can you?"

I tapped my right index finger on the table, the way that my second grade teacher used to do when she was upset with her little urchins that pretended to be students.

"I think that you've got a nice looking storefront, but I'm not sure who is managing the business, if you get what I mean. You're right, I just can't figure you out."

"And what is it that you can't figure out?" she said.

"All right. Here's for starters—what was it between you and Davey? Were you lovers, or just friends?"

Vickie lifter her chin the way Godzilla used to in the cheap flicks when he was about ready to flame-breath a city.

"That is the burning question about me that keeps you awake at night?" she sneered.

"I'm a lonely guy," I said.

"I wouldn't have thought that you were that lonely."

"Yeah, well, can you just answer the question?"

"Davey never told you?" she countered.

"If he had, would I bother to ask you?"

She nodded, and I could feel the machinery of her mind whirring and clicking.

"Well?" I persisted.

"Davey was in love with me," she said finally.

"That much I knew. But how did you feel about him?"

"He was a friend. That's all."

She said it simply, the way that most people would say that they had an aquarium stocked with carp.

"Bullshit."

"He was my cover as well, if you have to know."

"From who? Your father? An old boyfriend?"

"Hardly," she laughed. "I'm a lesbian."

Okay. She was a lesbian. So what? It wasn't anything to me, except that I wished that I didn't find her physically attractive.

"Surprised?" she asked.

It was a test, I thought, and a stupid one; she was looking for some stereotyped response so that she could lecture me on how narrow minded that I was.

"I don't give a damn," I replied.

"Funny, the way that your pants stretch when you're around me, I thought that you cared a lot."

"Dream on, Vickie."

I didn't mean it.

"Not about you, I won't."

"Then how about telling me who it was that Davey was protecting you from. You know, having Davey as a cover is liking trying to shield yourself from an oncoming bullet with the Pillsbury Doughboy."

"Not quite," she said. "Davey was the only possible cover between myself and the person that I've been afraid of for the last few years. It wasn't his physique that qualified him for the job."

"Then what was it?" I asked. "His outstanding ability to con people?"

"No, Jason. Davey was supposed to protect me from a hired killer who has no conscience. A man who was, until recently, at the top of his profession. This man considers himself above the law; he is a man who is, in my opinion, without remorse or mercy."

"Davey was supposed to shield you from a stone cold killer, is that it?"

She nodded once.

"Lady, you picked the wrong guy to be your cover."

"No," she said solemnly. "Davey was the only person in the world that his man seemed to have affection or friendship for, and that was why Davey volunteered to help us."

"Us?" I asked.

"Your sister and I."

"My sister was in danger? What in the hell has been going on?" I demanded. "Why would my sister be in danger? Who is this asshole that the two of you were worried about?"

"Your sister was never in danger, Jason," she said. "But she was worried about what could happen to me."

"Who were the two of you afraid of?" I persisted.

She looked around the restaurant the way Billy always did when he was trying to surprise an eavesdropper, although I have to admit that she pulled it off with a lot more class.

"We were," she admitted, when she returned her attention to me, "both afraid of you."

I couldn't believe what I was hearing.

"Me?" I asked. "Why in the hell would you be afraid of me?"

A split second before she answered, I knew the answer.

"Because," she said, "up until the day she died, your sister and I were lovers. She thought that you would kill me if you found out."

Vickie Matisse, the gorgeously beautiful lesbian, watched me as though waiting for me to exhibit signs of masculine self-righteousness such as reaching across the table and slapping the living shit out of her, or maybe pulling the Beretta from its shoulder holster and shooting her in the throat. She didn't have a clue either. My sister and I had had a complicated relationship, and I didn't give a damn whether she had slept with Vickie Matisse or not. I did care that my sister thought that I would have killed Vickie if I had found out.

My sister Diedre was the first woman that I had ever slept with, although she had been only thirteen years old at the time. No one ever knew that it happened except the two of us. My first reaction after Vickie had told me was not that I should kill her for what had occurred, but fear that they had been close enough that Diedre had told Nat Matisse' daughter what had happened.

You do things when you're young that are inalterably stupid. Sometimes they just happen. Our parents had never told either of us anything about sex. We had experimented on our own. It just happened that it had been with each other. We were, you see, left alone together a lot. I'm not excusing what occurred. I can't. It just happened. I don't really know how or why, but I've felt guilty about it ever since. It felt good, but it was bad according to the "rules."

I think that after it happened, the guilt started eating at me so much that, combined with what I went through in Viet Nam, I turned into a relatively heartless prick. Contract enforcement was a natural for me. If I hadn't fell into the thing with Lydia Retkin when I returned from the war, I would have made one hell of a gangster. I think that I would have given Vickie's old man a run for the money.

"I'm not going to kill you, Vickie. I don't give a shit. If anybody had asked me while this was all going on, I would have told you the same thing then. Diedre's life was her business. Your life's your business. What pisses me off is why anyone would think that I would kill anybody over this."

But the truth was that I had hated every man that Diedre had ever been with. I had told myself that it was because they weren't good enough for her; and I truly didn't think that they were. The thing was that Diedre had been convinced that I was jealous of them. She thought that I loved her, which I did, but as a lover, not as a brother. There was, I have to admit, a small grain of truth in what she thought, but, in the main, I was past that kind of thinking. I'm not proud of what happened between us, but, like I said, it happened. It was over.

I wondered again if she had told Vickie. I searched her face for any indication, but saw none.

"I know things about you, Jason. Things that you have done."

I didn't like where I thought that she was going.

"My father says that you poured gasoline on a man and burned him to death while his hands were handcuffed behind his back."

She was pressing ahead where she had no right to press. I didn't like where she was going, but I was intrigued as to why she was taking me there. In all the time that I had known Vickie, we had never really had a direct conversation about anything other than the weather.

"That would be Vinnie," I said. "He deserved it."

"And my father said that you forked a man to death. Stabbed him to death with a table fork."

"That would be Marty," I said defensively. And that would be the night that I flipped out so badly that even though I was sleeping with Lydia Retkin at the time, she had had me retired. Not just retired, institutionalized as well. At least Lydia had me locked away in an institution with decent food, unlike the Army when they put me away in the coat with the backwards arms for a year or so.

"He deserved it too, I suppose."

I didn't answer. She obviously had preconceived notions.

"But it wasn't what you did, he said, it was how you did it. He said you were cold. That you didn't get any enjoyment out of it. You didn't do it out of rage. You just did it to get it done with, but that for some reason you took your time. My father says that when you kill a man, if you don't get a rush—good or bad—out if it, that there's something wrong with you. He says that you don't get a rush. He says that he thinks it's because you carry a dead man inside of you."

"Since when did you start listening to your father? You know that he's a psychopath." I said.

"I've always listened to him when he talked about you, Jason. You're a special case. Think about it—you're own sister said that you would kill me, and she loved you. What kind of a man terrifies his own sister?"

"Like you're not afraid of your own father? Listen to yourself."

"I'm not afraid of my father," she said. "I hate him, but I have to live with that. And I know what he is, but I have a hard time figuring out who or what you are."

"Who I am," I said, "is not the same man that I was a couple of years ago."

CHAPTER 6

"Something big is going on," Billy was saying to me. I had the car phone on speaker again.

"Just tell me what it is, Billy, I'm having a bad damn day."

Nothing ever good, I had decided, ever came from spending time with Vickie Matisse.

"Well, maybe this will make it better," he said. "There's a hunt going on. Major league. You better get your ass to Toronto before it's over."

I was weaving and dodging the potholes on Michigan Avenue on the way to my hotel room, and I thought that at least Canada had better roads, and that I could use a trip to calm down from my meeting with Vickie. "A hunt? What kind of a hunt? Who's hunting, Billy, and what are they hunting for?"

"You're not going to believe this, man," said Billy. His voice was charged with excitement to the point that I thought I could feel it over the phone. "Have you ever heard of Dr. Stanley Rathbone?"

"Never," I said, "but let me guess—he works for Traxor, right?"

"Worked for Traxor," corrected Billy. "His job description now reads dead—as in doornail."

"He died in the Traxor explosion?"

"Right on, boss. Dr. Rathbone was incinerated when the Traxor labs blew up. He was the one that Davey was on the phone with when fireworks happened."

I was so intent on what he was saying that I didn't see an upcoming crater, but I felt it when the car jolted as though it had been nearly missed by a mortar.

"Son of a bitch," I yelled.

"Damn right," said Billy. "And here's another son of a bitch. Dr. Rathbone was the point man on the hunt."

"Are you going to tell me what it is that Traxor is hunting for?" I asked irritably.

"Some advanced program that he was responsible for. What do you think of that?" he asked.

"Cool," I said, "but you're not making a lot of sense. Why did somebody nuke the doc if he was doing his job?"

"Because," said Billy, with a touch of real pride in his voice, "they found out at Traxor that Dr. Rathbone had hidden the program for his own reasons and was just pretending to be looking for it. In reality, he was throwing them red herrings."

"Great," I said. "But what's this all got to do with Davey?"

"I don't know," he admitted as I was pulling into the parking lot for the Ritz Carlton.

"Did they have a name for this 'advanced program'?" I asked.

"Sure did. It was called Spider. Now is that worth a bonus or what?"

"Say that again?"

"Spider."

A light green Saturn was dogging my tail, trying to pass me, and I slowed down to let it go by. The driver, a longhaired Hunter Thompson clone with sunglasses, thrust his middle finger up to show me what he thought of my driving. Within a fifteen mile radius of Detroit, that gesture is considered a sign of affection.

"This is getting more interesting as it goes," I said.

"It's getting me more nervous by the minute, Jason," he replied. "I've got this creepy feeling that someone's been watching me. If I didn't know better, I'd swear that someone has been creeping around the insides of my computer."

"Well, have they or haven't they?" I asked.

"I don't know, maybe I'm being paranoid. There's just something that I can't put my finger on that's different about the way that it operates. Maybe we should lie off of this 'Spider' thing for a while. I've got a wife and kids, man, and I can't have anything happen to them. You run single, and that's cool, but I've got family. If somebody tags me, I'm a sitting duck."

"Calm down, Billy," I said, "spend a few hours in that wood shop of yours. Turn a few lathes, soothe your nerves."

"That's it?" he demanded. "That's your best advice? How about you put an armed guard to watch my house? How about that?"

"I'll think about it," I said. "They can't be that close yet. I'll think about it."

"Do more than think about it," he said.

"Okay, I'll take care of it," I said, trying to calm him down. "You know," I continued, "when this is all over, why don't you show me your wood shop? I've never seen one before."

"Sure thing, Jason," he snorted. "I'm sure you'll come to visit right after hell freezes over. You've got to look after me, man, I've got family and this Spider thing is starting to give me arachnophobia. The people looking for this are starting to spook me big time. I'm sending the family away until things cool down. I don't want one of my kids hurt."

"What's really humorous," I told Billy as though the subject was closed, "is that I know where Spider is. An anonymous caller left me a message."

"You do? Where?"

I was one-upping Billy, and I think I had offended his professional pride. I don't think that he liked it. His questions had come a little too quickly, and I could hear the irritation in his voice.

"In the web," I said.

I pulled into a vacant parking spot only a mile or two from the main entrance to the hotel.

"In the web?" asked Billy. "Where the hell is that?"

"I don't have a clue," I said, and turned off both the ignition and Billy at the same time.

Mrs. Alderton was not in a good mood. She was on the phone when I entered my room, but she nonetheless greeted me with the barrel of her Beretta pointing at my throat instead of explaining what the hell she was doing in my room. Most people aim for a body shot. Mrs. Alderton had a more refined sense of aim. Throat shots were a specialty of hers.

She was sitting in a cushioned chair behind a cherry wood desk her lower torso hidden behind a laptop computer, and motioned me with the barrel of her gun towards the other of the two chairs at the table.

"I understand," she was saying into the phone.

She was wearing a light blue cotton-jogging suit. Most days, Mrs. A. ran at least five miles, an exercise to which she attributed her amazing stamina and physical fitness. As I walked toward her, I thought that looked like any other old lady pointing a Beretta at me. She looked dangerous.

"How long have you known this?" she asked the nameless somebody on the other end of the phone. There was an edge to her voice that I had never heard before. The afternoon light reflected off of her eyes like sharp flashes from signal mirrors.

"Give the source," she said matter-of-factly, after the lag time of a response from the other end that I couldn't hear.

She listened for a few moments, staring at me all the while as though she would like to pistol whip me, and then hung up the phone without saying good-bye.

"I'd say that you were having the same kind of day that I am," I said, flashing her a half smile.

"You," she said, "are a pain in my ass."

"Thank you, I think."

"Don't back talk me, Jason Sulu. Didn't I tell you to leave well enough alone?"

"You didn't say it like you meant it, Mrs. A.," I said.

"Kids," she snorted.

"Yeah," I agreed.

"How much do you already know?" she asked.

"Can I have those chocolates on your bed before I spill my guts?" I asked her in return.

"Chow down, boy toy," she said.

I walked over to her bed and grabbed the chocolates. On the way there, I considered whether to be straight with her or not. I knew, or at least was reasonably sure, that Mrs. Alderton and I were on the same end of somebody's gun, and that we were therefore theoretically allies.

"While you're thinking, dear boy," she admonished, "keep this in mind. You already need more friends than you have if you want to last out the week."

As calmly as I could, I peeled back the green foil from the chocolate mints that had been lying on her bed, and popped them in my mouth. They tasted unaccountably flat, and for a brief moment I wondered whether or not I had just swallowed poison intended for Mrs. Alderton.

"They taste like shit, don't they?" she asked. "But don't worry, they're not poisoned. Now quit stalling, sit down, and tell me what you know. And don't bullshit me. I already know that you've had Bumper and the bitch queen working overtime."

So I did. I told her the whole shooting match, except for the private bit about my sister and I and the message about the spider and the web. Mrs. Alderton took it all in without saying a word or asking a question until I was completely through.

Mechanically, she reached for her coffee cup, tilted it back and took a drink of what looked to be seriously room temperature Java.

"Here's the way it is, Jason. I'm going to break rank and fill in some blanks for you.

"Second," she continued without missing a beat, "you want to know why Davey let your sister die. The answer is that she wanted it that way. You're sister was even more screwed up than you are, Jason, and she just couldn't live with herself. It's a bitch, but it's a fact. It was bound to happen sooner or later; I'm surprised that you hadn't figured that out for yourself a long time ago. Bisexual bimbos don't have much stability in their lives. Sorry, I don't give a damn about the valid lifestyle bullshit and the personal choice crap. David Bowie and Elton John didn't design this world that we live in. The straights have it. You want to live a normal life, play by the rules. You want to join a sex cult, have at it, but live or die by the consequences. End of sermon."

Anger had begun to smolder in my brain. Diedre was not a freak, and her sexual choices were her own business. Without realizing it until after I had done it, I clenched and unclenched my right hand.

"Are we okay here, sport?" asked Mrs. Alderton. Her Beretta was pointing at me again, this time with a purpose. Her hand, in spite of her age, was steady as always.

"Fine," I said.

Would she kill me if I wasn't fine?

"I'll take you at your word, Jason," she said, but she kept the Beretta aimed at my heart. "The next thing you probably want to know is who killed Davey. Am I right?"

I didn't answer; her brutal assessment of my sister and her lifestyle had caused a small emotional overload.

"Forget your sister, Jason. I didn't mean to be the wicked witch, but I've never pulled punches with you because I've grown fond of you, and I won't start now when you need me to be to the point. Everybody else thinks that you a bomb with a burning fuse. Your psychological profile is not healthy, my friend. If you hadn't been operating in a world where psychopathologies were valuable when tightly controlled, you would have been institutionalized a long time ago. And if you hadn't been screwing Lydia Retkin, son, you would have been retired at the very least "with extreme prejudice," as they say."

"Billy Bumper," I pointed out, "says that I'm an asshole."

"Well, he hasn't spent a lot of time around me, has he Jason?"

"No," I admitted.

"So anyway," she continued, "as to exactly who killed Davey, I'm going to tell you the one hundred percent complete and total truth, if you can handle it. Can you?"

It's hard to explain how I get when I'm losing it. I feel separated from reality, as though I'm looking into our own dimension through a convex portal that is slightly fogged so that I can see nothing at all very clearly. I feel slightly flushed; perhaps it's only in my mind, but it feels as though my body temperature goes up a few degrees. And my hands clench and unclench, clench and unclench automatically until I'm over it.

Sometimes, I feel burning in my throat, as though the valve at the top of my esophagus isn't working, and the stomach acid is erupting up and into my throat. Other times, I feel this incredible sense of avenging power, as though adrenaline were rushing through my body. I usually hear the Dark Voice.

I got it under control in time, though. I hadn't lost it since Lydia retired me, although I have to admit that Mrs. Alderton's gun assisted my thinking.

"I can handle it," I said with an effort.

"Here it is, then. I don't have a clue. My people don't have a clue. Lydia doesn't have a clue, and the Nat Matisse is saying that he doesn't have a clue."

"He claims he doesn't have a clue, just like me" I said, emphasizing the word claim. "So, would you mind finally telling me who it is that you work for? I can keep a secret."

"No."

Her mouth was pinched together, her eyes, as usual, still stared directly into my own.

"Can I make a guess?"

"Why bother?"

She had a point, but I wasn't going to let that stop me.

"I'd say that you're working for a consortium these days. Officially, that is."

"And?"

"I'd say in reality that you're still working for the same deep, dark government agency that you used to, but that neither Lydia Retkin nor Nat Matisse know that for sure. How am I doing so far?"

"You're getting in deeper," she replied.

"And here's another guess," I continued. "I'll bet that you really don't know everything that's going on with the consortium, and that you're getting concerned."

She could have raised her gun, shot me, and got it over with. With the kind of horsepower that Mrs. Alderton had backing her, she would have got away with it clean. My death wouldn't even have shown up in the obituaries. "Maybe," I said, "you're the one who needs some help. Size up who it is that you've been working with, and maybe you'll start to feel as outnumbered as I do."

"And you think that everything will be all right if I just team up with you?" she snapped back. "Wake up, Jason. Nothing is all right or will be all right unless Spider is found."

"I told you, if you'll tell me what it is, I'll tell you where it's at. It's a straight deal."

It was, too, except that I hadn't verified the information. However, I had to admit that I didn't know what the phone message meant.

"How in the hell can you know where Spider is if you don't know what Spider is? Give me a break, Jason."

So I told her about the message, but not the content.

"Did the caller identify themselves?" she asked.

"No," I replied. "The voice was electronically masked so well that it didn't even sound human, so there's no clue there."

Her reaction surprised me. She actually tilted her head and opened her mouth. In all the years that I had known, Mrs. Alderton, I had never seen her gape in amazement.

"No," she said softly.

"Yes," I said. "It was mechanical sounding, like one of those damn automated operators that the phone company uses, only worse."

"Think hard," she said, leaning forward so far that the tips of her breast actually touched the table. "This is very important. Did the voice sound at all human?"

"I don't understand what the problem is here. I told you that it was electronically masked."

"Did you save the answering sound file?"

"Sure," I said. "It was on the computer that blew our house to smithereens.

Her fingers curled into a tight ball, her fist raised high, and she slammed her senior citizen fist onto the table so hard that coffee spilled out from her half full cup.

"Damnation," she said.

"Mrs. A., what's the big damn deal? I told you; it wasn't something that you could run a voice ID from, anyway. Now are you going to tell me about Spider, or not?"

"Where, Jason? Tell me where it is." "What about tit for tat? That was the deal, remember?"

I was smiling, thinking things were starting to go my way when I saw the metallic circle that was the end of her gun pointing straight at my throat. Her eyes were devoid of humor. What I noticed more than anything else, though, was that her fingers were a shade whiter than normal. Her grip was professionally loose, but she was ready to fire.

"Down to that, Mrs. A.?" I asked quietly.

"You just don't what you've gotten involved in," she said. "Now tell me straight—where is Spider?"

"What is Spider?" I exploded. "What kind of damn computer program is worth killing me over? Why is it so fucking important? Exactly how many billions of dollars is this program worth?"

"Tell me where it is."

"Go ahead, pull the trigger," I said. "Then where will you be?"

"At your funeral."

"It's the only trump card that I have, I said, "and I'm not giving it away for free."

The phone rang.

Mrs. Alderton and I continued our face-off. Her gun never wavered. It probably never would until she hit her eighties.

The phone rang again. After the third ring, Mrs. Alderton, picked up the phone.

I screwed my face up and cocked my whole head to the side as an inquiry.

"Who?" I mouthed.

But she wasn't seeing me. Whoever was on the phone had her full attention.

Finally, she refocused on me, laid the gun on the table, and put her hand over the mouthpiece.

"It's for you," she whispered.

"Who is it?" I whispered back, forgetting for the moment that she was going to blow my brains out a few seconds ago.

"Spider," she said, with a look of utter amazement on her face. I took the phone from her outstretched hand, shook it gently loose from her grip, and said "hello" into the mouthpiece, but I heard only a dial tone.

"I think you waited too long," I said, passing the phone back to her.

Mrs. Alderton nodded.

"I think that we'd better get out of this room," she said, suddenly serious.

I was only an inch out of my chair when the phone rang again.

CHAPTER 7

"Don't answer that," snapped Mrs. Alderton.

I froze.

"You want to stay here?" I asked.

She looked at me, and suddenly she looked another year old with indecision.

"Screw it," she said, mustering back some of her normal decisiveness. "Let's get out of here."

Mrs. Alderton led the way into the hall, and kept straight on going for the elevators. The doors hissed shut behind us and we began our descent. I tensed, waiting for the deja vu explosion that never happened.

"Your car?" she said as we walked as quickly as we could toward the front door to get out of the building.

"East side parking lot," I said back. "Near the edge of the lawn."

She nodded, and kept up her brisk pace.

"What the hell is going on?" I asked when we got to the car.

"Get in and start driving," she said, letting out a short, hard breath. "I'll tell you once we're on the road."

She took her time about it, not saying a word until we hit the Southfield freeway. Her gun was in her purse, and I thought that I was pretty well out of danger for a while.

"Just keep your eyes on the road," she said. "I've changed my mind. I'm going to tell you about Spider."

I didn't respond, not wanting to give her any reason at all to hesitate. Cars passed us on both the left and the right as I waited for her to begin. The afternoon was fading, and I knew that we had at most another thirty minutes of daylight.

"Spider's not a computer program, Jason," she said. "It's something entirely different. At first we thought that it was a program, an AI program, but that was just another of our ongoing screw-ups, perhaps the smallest of the many errors that we made."

She lapsed into silence for a moment before continuing.

"You've heard of the Seti program?" she asked.

"No," I said. "Should I be?"

"The Seti program was a classified investigation," she said, ignoring my response, "into the possibility that mankind was receiving messages from extraterrestrials, but that we just didn't understand the method of communication. You must know that our own government bombards outer space constantly with a electronic messages prepared using technologies in the hope that an extraterrestrial civilization will receive and decode them so that our cultures can establish communication."

"I don't know shit about that kind of stuff," I said, "and I'm glad that I don't."

"At any rate," she said, ignoring my response yet again, "our government also analyzes electromagnetic radiation that bombards the earth. The "white noise of the heavens", as it's called, in the hope that we are receiving messages. We have scientists working day and night around the clock on their computers, looking for anything that remotely resembles an alien communication. Only computers have the number-crunching horsepower to handle the task."

"Go on," I urged, but I was beginning to get either pissed or confused since I couldn't see the relevance of what she was telling me to anything called "Spider."

"To 'protect' some of what was going on from the prying eyes of the American public, Traxor Corporation was formed in Canada. It was—you were right—a three-way consortium. Lydia brought old money and power; Matisse brought 'clean' muscle and certain…connections. But neither of those are important anymore, Jason. Nothing is important compared to what happened.

"What happened is this—a scientist at Traxor who was processing electromagnetic data stumbled across something so incredible that it literally brought any other considerations to a screeching halt."

We were going southbound on M-39, heading just anywhere so that we could talk. The darkening skies looked as though they held some promise of rain, and I remember thinking that I wished that it would rain, just so that I could smell the cool, crisp spring air when the storm was over.

"What did the geek find?" I asked.

"Something totally unexpected; something that they could never have foreseen."

"Like what?" I asked. "I don't mean to be impatient, but we've only got a quarter tank of gas, and if this is going to take awhile, then maybe I should stop and get fuel."

I stole a quick glance at her. She was definitely not amused.

"We found life."

"Excuse the hell out of me, Mrs. Alderton, but you mean someone's been trying to kill me because our government found extraterrestrial life? And what exactly does that have to do with Davey being murdered?"

"We found life," she said, "but it wasn't extraterrestrial."

"You found life on earth? Wonderful—and here I thought that you and I were alone on this planet."

I should have been more understanding, but I wasn't in the mood to be jived, even by Mrs. Alderton.

"Jason, I have the feeling that you think this old lady is bullshitting you, but I'm not, I'm really not. The scientist analyzing the patterns found life, but not in the electromagnetic scatter from space."

"Okay, I give," I said, "where exactly did he or she find it?"

"In the Internet," she replied.

"Where else?" I said. "I mean, aliens in the Internet, now I understand everything."

"Shut up and drive," she snapped.

"Any place in particular? I've got a dinner date."

"With Dr. Corey?"

"Marianne. She lets me call her Marianne since we're on such good terms. And how do you know so much about my private life?"

"You don't have a private life," she said, "so I'll go with you. Dr. Corey can finish the explanations. You may find her more convincing. If, that is, you think that you can handle two women at dinner…"

I couldn't, but I nodded anyway. It was going to be both an interesting and a long night.

Dr. Corey, who was dressed in a body-hugging black cotton dress, was not happy to see Mrs. Alderton, even though Mrs. Alderton had stopped and changed into navy blue slacks and a corded white angora sweater. We had gone back to her hotel room briefly to accomplish this change. There had been no calls from 'Spider,' and Mrs. A. had refused to discuss the earlier attempt at contact. Mrs. Alderton had changed in less than ten minutes and we have left immediately to meet Dr. Corey. Her quick change had gotten us to the restaurant twenty minutes early. You'd think that the doctor would have appreciated the effort.

We were sitting in a corner alcove behind an octagonal glass and would phone booth that was about five feet away from us. An olive skin man who looked fresh from the Mediterranean had left the booth just as we were sitting down. He was about six inches taller than me, putting him somewhere around six foot four, and had a full head of black hair that was salon perfect. His tan suit was elegantly cut and must have set him back a grand or so. I watched him head straight from the booth and out of the door. He was moving a little too quickly, and I thought briefly about going after him and retrieving him, but then decided that I was getting a little too paranoid.

"I don't think that this is a good idea," Dr. Corey told Mrs. Alderton, after the waiter had taken our order.

"I didn't ask," said Mrs. A.

"She never asks," I explained.

"Let's cut the crap, shall we?" said Mrs. Alderton. "I've got things to do, and Marianne, things have changed considerably since the last time that we spoke. Jason needs to be in the loop now. It's not a request, it's an order."

"I don't report to you," said Dr. Corey in a huff.

"The order is not from me, but I'd advise you to comply," replied Mrs. Alderton.

"And if I don't?"

"Well, dear, if you don't, then I'll need to check the records for a list of your next of kin so that we can notify them."

People can gulp, I saw Dr. Corey do it. It was more of a spasmed swallow if you want to get technical about it, but gulped describes it well enough. She was looking nervously at me when she did it, as though she thought Mrs. Alderton was saying that she didn't talk, and then I would hurt her. She obviously didn't know Mrs. Alderton like I did.

"But shouldn't I check first with…you know…shouldn't…" Dr. Corey stammered.

"You should do as you're told," said Mrs. Alderton, "and don't take all damned night about it. Tell Mr. Sulu about Spider."

"Well, what does he want to know?"

"Hey," I said, and snapped my fingers to get her attention, "I'm right here. You don't need to use Mrs. Alderton as a translator."

Dr. Corey's cheeks had flushed a deep red, and it flattered her face. I had noticed the tight dress, the fact that she wore lipstick, and had guessed that she had some idea of getting information from me using seduction as her extraction technique. She obviously didn't know me very well, either.

The waiter came and left behind the salads, which none of us touched. Dr. Corey stared at hers as though it were a religious offering from which she could draw strength. Her head was bowed as though praying. I risked a glance at Mrs. Alderton and saw that she was rubbing her right thumb and forefinger together, which was the only nervous habit I had ever known her to exhibit. Whether it meant that she was thinking, getting irritated, or something entirely different I had never been able to divine. Maybe her thumb just itched.

Eventually Dr. Corey looked up at me and batted her eyes. Anita Allison did it much better, I thought.

"What is it that you want to know, Mr. Sulu?" she asked. "You can call me Jason, and I want to know what Spider is, with no prompting or questions directed to Mrs. Alderton. Okay?"

"But that information is classified, Mr.—Jason."

"Permit me one more point, Jason," inserted Mrs. Alderton. When I nodded, she continued. "Dr. Corey, we have an emergency here. Spider has tried to contact Mr. Sulu."

"What?" Dr. Corey gaped at Mrs. Alderton. "That can't be. How? Why? Why would Spider try to contact someone that it doesn't know? And how? What do you mean trying to contact Mr. Sulu? By what means."

"By telephone and through his computer," said Mrs. Alderton.

"Oh my God, we have a chance to—."

"That'll do, dear. Now tell Jason what Spider is. He already knows the broad strokes of how it was found, but I want you tell him what Spider is."

It took Dr. Corey a few minutes to digest what she had learned, and she played with her hair a lot as she thought things through. The problem with classified information is that regular people don't want to go to jail for divulging it. As a result, they hem and haw and try to find ways to get past yakking about it until they have no other choice. Mrs. Alderton had obviously threatened and maneuvered Dr. Corey into that position because she eventually opened up.

"Spider is a new life form," she said.

"From outer space, right?" I asked derisively.

"No. Is that what you thought?" Dr. Corey shot Mrs. Alderton a confused look.

"Just answer the question," I said.

"All right," she said. "You don't have to be so rude. Spider is a new life form that has appeared within the world's telecommunications network. We don't specifically know how it appeared or when or why, but we know that it exists. Right now, the problem is that we don't know where exactly it is within that network. Our best guess is that is somewhere within the Internet."

Mrs. Alderton raised an eyebrow at me and I shrugged. I wasn't impressed. There's not much difference between the truth and a well rehearsed lie unless you know which questions to ask.

"This sounds like bullshit to me, Dr. Corey," I said. "For starters, what exactly is this 'life form'? Are we talking a pure energy creature here like they use in the sci-fi movies and books? Make some effort to convince me here before I get mad. I'm used to people lying to me, but you don't have to make such a production out of it."

Her back stiffened with anger, and it caused her breasts to thrust forward slightly. She had that "don't screw with the Queen of the Nile" posture.

"I'm not lying to you, Mr. Sulu," she said archly, forgetting that we were now on a first name basis. "Spider is real. It is a genuinely new life form the like of which, as far as we know, has never before existed. It is intelligent. It can think and, it can communicate."

"And," I added, "it lives in computers."

It was sarcasm on my part, but she nodded enthusiastically.

"Yes, it lives in computers, and in telephone lines, and perhaps in radio waves, and—."

"Get a hold of yourself, doctor, you sound like you're heading straight off of the deep end without a parachute."

"You don't believe any of this, do you?" she asked. Although it doesn't see that much use these days, the word "flabbergasted" described her reaction better than anything else.

"Jason is a special case, dear," intoned Mrs. Alderton. "He's esoterically challenged."

"But this is the most exciting event in the history of the world," bubbled Dr. Corey. "You have to believe me, Mr. Sulu."

"I don't have to believe shit, lady," I said. "I'm in this to find out who killed Davey Wiltz, remember? I don't care if you found alien burritos living in your computers. I think that you're feeding me a line of crap, and I'm already tired of hearing it."

"I am a respected scientist," she said, "and I have ethical standards."

"Are you the same woman scientist who's banging her married boss?

Are you? Because if you are, then maybe your ethical standards are compromised already. If you are, then maybe you don't have ethical standards; you just do what feels good for you. So, maybe you'll excuse me for doubting that you're so much of a Girl Scout that you always tell the truth. You see, I don't know just how much I can depend on you."

"Jason—."

"Let me finish, Mrs. A—. I was just—."

Her eyes caught mine, and then dropped; so I looked down to see her finger pointing toward the phone booth.

"Maybe I am getting old," she said pointedly.

"Maybe I'm getting senile," I said.

"What are you two talking about?" asked Dr. Corey.

There wasn't anything out of the ordinary that I could see about the phone booth. It was just glass and wood with a pay phone inside. The man that had been inside it had left as soon as we arrived, but that could have been a coincidence—that's what I had put it down to, but what if I had been wrong? I was thinking just that when I noticed the screwdriver on top of the phone. It must have shaken him up when we arrived early, jarred him into making a stupid little mistake. Even professionals make little mistakes, but, honestly, it was the first time that I had seen one leave a screwdriver lying around.

"I said," said Dr. Corey, "what are the two of you talking about?"

The phone booth was not the best place to put a bomb. The table that we were sitting at would have been better. This would presuppose that we were to be steered to the table we were at. Also, a bomb would have taken out Dr. Corey and her clinging black dress, and, although I wasn't naive enough to believe that whoever would have planted a bomb there would be overly concerned about her dying, my gut said that it wasn't a bomb.

Mrs. Alderton didn't think that it was either, or she would have been on her way out the back door. I trusted her instincts more than my own. She may have been older than me, but at least she wasn't retired. That left bugging devices—maybe a hair-thin fiber optic thrown in for good measure.

"First, you insult me," said Dr. Corey, leaning over the table as though to bite my head off, "which you have no right to do, and then you ignore me. Any relationship that I might have with Dr. Meshke is none of your business. I don't know who that you think you are, but if Dr. Meshke finds out what you've been saying, I think that you'll regret it. Are you paying attention to me?"

I was giving the phone booth most of my attention, which is how I missed the shooter. He was somewhere back in the hallway behind Mrs. Alderton, so I can't fault her. She's good, but she doesn't have eyes in the back of her head.

Silencers do make noise, contrary to their name and popular belief, but I missed it over the hubbub in the restaurant. When I saw the bloody hole appear in Dr. Corey's forehead and saw her head jerk back, however, I pulled my gun out from beneath my coat and dropped to my one knee and fired two rounds down the hallway. When the percussion of the shots had died away, the rest of the restaurant had either gone quiet or I had gone deaf.

There was no return fire, and I was debating whether to take another shot just to be sure, when Mrs. Alderton turned to me and said pointedly, "Can't you ever leave someone alive so that I can question them?"

"It's a bad habit," I agreed.

CHAPTER 8

❀

*M*rs. Alderton got stuck with the job of cleaning up the mess. It's her job, and I couldn't handle it anyway. With Dr. Corey shot dead right at the dining table and a total stranger dead in the hallway, the place was out of control. People were screaming and the manager passed out cold when he saw Dr. Corey's body. I couldn't handle that. I don't think that Mrs. Alderton particularly liked dealing with a frightened mob, but she could do it. I had somewhere else to be.

It was dark outside when I got into the car and hit the road. That had happened to me a lot over the years, or maybe I just noticed it more than most people. I'd go inside somewhere when it was still light outside, but when I left again, somebody had pulled a blanket over the sun.

I tried Billy on my car phone, but there was no answer at his place. Maybe he was taking care of relocating his wife and kids to a relative or someplace else equally predictable. Maybe. I hoped that the little asshole was okay.

Anita answered her phone on the first ring. She was still at the office, working hard, trying to take the bonus for getting me what I wanted to know from Billy.

"I've got some good stuff for you, Jason," she said.

"Don't talk," I said quickly. "I think we're marked and being tracked. Dr. Corey just took a bullet in the head right while I was having dinner with. Stay where you are, I'm on my way to your office for a chat."

It wasn't much of a code. Anita and I had used it for years. It meant get the hell out quick, and do what you have to do to meet me at Elizabeth Park in the ice skating shelter, and don't go home before you do. Anita may have been kinky when it came to her sex life, but she knew how to handle herself. Sometimes, though, that's not enough.

I tried Billy on the phone again. There was still no answer. I had a bad feeling about it. He had nagged me on the phone, but he had been genuinely spooked; nervous enough to clear his family out of town. If things hadn't happened so quickly when I had gone back to my hotel room, I would have gone and checked on him.

As I drove to Trenton, towards Elizabeth Park, I felt keenly the lack of an organization behind me. When I had worked for Lydia, there were always other resources to deploy when I needed them. Maybe I was in over my head, trying to dig into something so obviously dangerous without the backing to see it through. Mrs. Alderton had told me to stay away from it, but I had ignored her. Ignoring Mrs. Alderton was generally a mistake.

I was halfway to Trenton, passing Eureka on Telegraph Road, when it began to piece together what Billy, Mrs. Alderton, and then Dr. Corey had begun to tell me. I had heard what they had all been saying, but it just hadn't really sunk in. Billy had told me that Spider was an artificial intelligence program worth big money. Mrs. Alderton had told me that Spider was a new life form discovered living within telecommunication networks. Maybe it was both. Since I didn't know much about technology, I had let it all slide mentally, waiting for the truth to shake out. By the time that I got to West Road and Eureka and turned left to take West Road to Jefferson, I was getting a major headache. I was beginning to believe that the key to unraveling the whole mess was Davey.

What I knew for sure was that if Davey was involved, that there was a major scam he was pulling. What I didn't know was how Davey had gotten involved in the first place. Suddenly, I had the answer. Davey had found out about Spider from Vickie Matisse. It had to have been the way it had happened. Her father Nat was part of the Traxor Consortium, and either Vickie knew about Spider, or he had tagged it through Nat. Davey probably met Nat through Vickie.

Nat Matisse would not have been happy knowing that his daughter was a lesbian, and that was the reason that she had run with Davey. So, she would have had to introduce Davey to keep daddy off of her back. Nat had a new venture with Lydia Retkin and the government agency that paid Mrs. Alderton. So far, so good.

But Nat didn't know anything about artificial intelligence programs, electronic life forms, or even how to play video games. I didn't know exactly why it was that Nat had been invited to or had forced his way into Traxor, but once in, he must have felt way over his head. He could have turned to his daughter's boyfriend for advice, since Davey had no doubt told him that his background was computer programming. It made sense. That would be how Davey got involved in the first place. From there, it had probably gotten out of control pretty quickly.

But even Davey would not have been naïve enough to try and con Nat Matisse. There were limits. So, he had to have found a mark within Traxor. It would have had to have been someone involved with Spider, whatever Spider really was. Dr. Meshke seemed to be the place to start, unless either Billy or Anita had someone in mind. A trip to Toronto seemed in order as soon as I made sure Billy and Anita were in the clear.

I would have to run the trip by Mrs. Alderton. She might know something that would make the trip to Canada unnecessary, but I doubted it. Besides, I didn't completely trust Mrs. Alderton's information sources. There was too much going on that she didn't seem to know about. For example, the men that had come to our house looking to take us out, the explosion that leveled the place, and the killing of Dr. Corey, Mrs. Alderton's masters, Lydia Retkin and her private army, or Nat Matisse and his "family"—it had to be one of those three main groups. All three of them were involved in my life, but only one had been involved with Davey's. Nat Matisse was beginning to look like he deserved a private visit.

I parked my car two blocks from the entrance to Elizabeth Park, in the parking lot of an apartment building that looked as if it had been built around the time of the Second World War. The night air was cool and bracing on my face, the way that an aftershave is supposed to be but never is.

Behind the apartment building was an open field that led to a drainage ditch that separated the park from the rest of the town. I cut across the field after picking up a small rock along the way and shoving it in my pocket, avoiding the sidewalks and the street lamps. There was no specific reason to expect trouble, but I felt better doing it.

As I walked, I tried to come to grips with why there was such a major crisis over either an AI program or a new life form. What was the big deal? Anita had let me know that AI was used in space and defense programs, with some commercial applications. I wondered if it could be tied to some new weapon or something along those lines, but speculation along those lines was just a waste of time without more information.

At least I could understand why people would be so brutal about it if there were military uses. If Spider was just a new life form, things were getting confusing. That would really be a case of "who cares?" Who in the hell would want to own a new life form? It wasn't like it was a new food group or anything.

I've never been proud of being shallow.

I followed the trees at the edge of the drainage ditch to the little stone walking bridge, which was roughly a quarter mile from the main entrance. Aside from being riskier to cross if it was being watched, the entrance bridge was closed off by two drop down steel railroad crossing type blockades.

From there, it was a twenty-minute walk to the ice skating shelter. I kept to the woods, skirting the one-way concrete road that wound through the park. When summer was in full swing, cars would line the road in the daytime teenager girls laying beside them on blankets and showing their wares with their boyfriends standing guard smoking cigarettes and daring you to look at their ladies. Kids would be playing baseball in the open field, shouting and urging their shirt sleeved friends on, and, at the ice cream stand, both adults and children would sit at picnic tables and drink pop and lick multicolor snow cones. But on that night, Elizabeth Park was a grim place.

The trees were like silent sentinels as I moved cautiously between them, undisturbed by my intrusion. They were, I imagine, standing guard against the night terrors that I had dreamed of as a boy or the Dark Judge who had counseled me as a man. There was enough moonlight that I could find my way, but not enough to move noiselessly.

I crossed one more stone bridge, crouching low as I traversed it. I would have felt foolish had I not seen Dr. Corey bite the bullet earlier. As careful as I was trying to be, though, someone with a night scope and a rifle would have had enough of a shot at me that I would have been dead. Either I was getting lucky, or, if someone had followed Anita, they had already come and gone. That was a thought as grim as the night itself.

The three skating rinks were in the wide-open field that was foreboding in the dim moonlight. They were giant graves in a forgotten cemetery.

Crossing the field to get to the skating shelter on the far side did not seem an intelligent approach, so I stuck to the tree line that followed the edge of the par. As I drew closer, the skating shelter looked like a dark mausoleum, but I knew from having been to the park as a kid that it was really just three plywood sheets and a slope-shingled roof. Inside, as I remembered it, would be a plank wood bench on each of the three walls for exhausted skaters to collapse onto to escape the cold and re-gather their strength.

I saw Anita's little red sports car parked in the gravel parking lot beyond the shelter, and kept my ears cocked for noise. She was there. If she made any noise, I wanted to hear it.

About five feet from the shelter, I took the Beretta from my shoulder holster, and, holding it in my left hand, took the rock from my pocket with my right hand and tossed it against the side of the shelter. It hit with a loud crack. I waited for Anita to respond—that was the way that we planned it—but there was no response.

There was no other way to play it, so I just walked up to the shelter and looked into the darkness inside.

"Anita?" I whispered.

The silence was beginning to get on my nerves.

As my eyes adjusted to the darkness, I saw a dark bundle in the left corner, leaning against the far wall.

"Anita?" I repeated.

Another one bites the dust, I thought.

Almost one cue, the moon came out from behind a cloud and bathed the inside of the shelter in a soft white light. The woman's hair was long and blond, and hung straight, with less life than she had. She had taken a few bullets to the face, so, whatever she once looked like, she looked worse at that moment.

Where the hell is Anita? I wondered.

Feeling like a ghoul, I felt around the dead woman's body for a purse or a wallet, but found nothing. Either she was a pro, or someone had taken her purse to slow down trackers.

Not good, not good…I thought.

There was nothing more to do, so I walked back out of the shelter, and looked around to see if I could see Anita, but I saw nothing except the three dark skating rinks that looked like graves.

Anita might have been wired a little crazy, but I didn't want anything bad to happen to her. We had had some moderately good times together.

"Jason?" I heard a tentative voice call.

It came from the middle skating rink, and it was Anita's voice.

"C'est moi," I said, breathing a sigh of relief.

She stood up slowly, her head searching from side to side as she did so, looking for trouble that I thought was no longer a threat.

"Your work," I asked, "or was the rag doll already in the shelter waiting for you when you got here?"

"The bitch was following me," she sneered. "It was a good thing you called."

"You okay?" I asked.

"Better than her," she said, jerking her head in the direction of the shed. "But my slacks are ripped to shit. Some asshole left a broken beer bottle laying in the skating rink."

"You cut bad?" I asked. The moon had disappeared behind the clouds again, and it was too dark to tell if she was bleeding much.

"I live," she said, putting her arm around my waist for support. "Let's get out of here."

"Deal," I said. "Let's go check on Bumper. I haven't been able to get him on the phone, and he might have had visitors too."

We drove Anita's car back to where I had parked mine so that she didn't have to walk and so we wouldn't have to leave her car where the police would find it and ticket it. Along the way, I had flipped the car light on and saw the three slices in her right leg, one of which still had a small shard of glass sticking out.

Anita's looked a lot older than she had when I had last seen her, stared out through the windshield and into the night. She was intent on looking at the night that I thought at first that she might be in shock.

"I've got a first aid kit in the car," I offered.

"Good."

"Are you feeling all right?" I asked.

"I'm not in shock, if that's what you're asking. I'm just pissed. I'm so damned mad I can't even feel the cuts."

There was no sense in pressing the issue; I've felt the same way before myself.

We didn't have time to go to a clinic, since I tried Billy on the car phone a few times and couldn't raise him. I had a bad feeling that something had happened to him. My intuitions were usually wrong, though, so I wasn't giving up hope.

Anita cleaned her cuts after cutting open her slacks a good twelve inches on her right leg. The wounds didn't look so bad after she mopped the blood up with some paper napkins that I had laying in the coffee carrier. Although she looked like a wounded vet after she finally bandaged them, I knew she was going to be fine. She would be pissed when the real pain set in, but she would be okay.

I left her in the car, parked two alleyways away from Billy's house. He lived in an older neighborhood. Newer suburbs don't have alleys. I was glad for them because I could move a less obviously than if I had had to slink down the sidewalks.

It took some grousing around to locate Billy's house from the alley, but I didn't bump into anyone. His house was the one with a garage almost as large as the house itself. The garage was where Billy did his woodworking, and I knew from what he had told me that that was where he spent most of his time while at home because, although he loved his family dearly, he couldn't stand to be around them.

The light was on in the garage, but the windows were curtained and I couldn't see inside. At first I thought Billy didn't have a phone in the garage, but then I remembered that I had talked to him once while he was in there working on a tie rack that he was making.

Since the light was on, though, I reasoned that he must be in the garage working. Maybe he had the ringer on the phone turned off so that he wouldn't be disturbed.

I listened at the door, but I didn't hear anything—no power tools, no talking, no nothing.

I knocked at the door, and no one answered.

I tried the handle, and, since it was unlocked, pushed the door in gently. It opened silently, on well-oiled hinges.

"Billy?" I said softly.

I saw a band saw, a lathe, a drill press and a lot of other woodworking paraphernalia like files and such, a power saw, and a body wearing Billy-type clothes on the floor. On the right hand, I saw Billy's ugly school ring.

William Bumper the Third was dead the hard way. Someone had cut off his head with his own power saw. His wood shop was splattered with blood; the wood shavings on the floor were soaked with it. I didn't waste time looking for clues as to who did it, there was no point. I just got the hell out via the same door that I had come in, so that I could make sure that Anita was okay. I didn't even bother to look for Billy's head. The Dark Judge would lead me to it eventually.

I felt sorry for his wife and kids—sorrier for Billy. Bodies were beginning to stack up around me, and I was starting to think that I would never know specifically who was behind it or exactly why.

As I stepped out into the cool night, I heard a siren from somewhere to my left piercing the heavy night air, and I wondered if the killer had obligingly called the police. It would be bad to be anywhere near Billy's place if they had, so I headed back behind the garage, hopped over the fence, and took off down the alley towards where I had parked the car.

The moon was by then a bright white globe suspended against a lampblack sky, and although it was nice to see where I was going, I would have preferred to be a little less visible myself.

Halfway to the car, I head a thrashing noise from the bushes to my left, and spun in that direction, dropping to a half crouch as I did so. I had my weapon drawn and aimed before the two cats came tumbling out onto the alley pavement, screeching and yowling and trying to claw each other's faces off.

I put my gun away, and high-tailed it back to the car. Anita was sound asleep in the front sleep.

When I opened the door and the light came on, she awoke with a start. "It's just me," I said.

"Sorry," she told me, "I haven't had a lot of sleep lately. I've been running down leads to beat Billy."

"Don't worry about it. Go back to sleep. I'll drive us to someplace safe."

"Billy's okay?"

She sat there expectantly in torn black slacks, the bandages on her right leg spotted with blood, wearing a black turtleneck sweater that was ripped at the elbow.

"Billy's dead," I told her.

"They're going to get all of us," she said, her lips barely opening as she spoke the words.

It was the slackness of her face, empty of expression that made her look older.

"Who's going to get all of us?" I asked.

"Traxor," she replied simply.

"You mean Nat Matisse, or Lydia's boys, or the government?"

"Take your pick. This is big, Jason. Bigger than I ever imagined. I would have never taken the job if I had known how big. I'm in bad shape for money, but this one isn't worth it. Business has been bad. I was ready to suck cock for money if something didn't come along to pay the bills, but I should have passed on this one."

"Sorry," I said simply. "We better go."

I was putting my seat belt on when she asked, "How are his wife and kids holding up?"

It hit me hard. I hadn't checked his house to see whether or not he had gotten his family to safety in time. For all I knew, they could be laying headless in his house right at that minute. I didn't want to know.

"We've got to get out of here, Anita," I said, "I heard sirens coming this way."

She looked at me as though waiting for me to say something, anything that would comfort her fears. I could have told her that the people involved didn't bother killing wives and kids, but I remembered Raphael Alvarado, and what Matisse had done to his family. I saw tears forming in the corner of her eyes.

"Are they alive?" she asked.

"I don't know," I said. "If they're dead or alive, we'll have to read about it one way or the other in the paper tomorrow. It should make the front page."

I depressed the gas pedal gently and nursed the car down the alley with the headlights off until we hit a safe street.

Mrs. Alderton wasn't thrilled when I brought Anita back to the room with me. Deadly pissed described the way that she reacted pretty well. She tried to make me feel guilty by telling me what a bloody mess that I had left her with at the restaurant, and how she barely kept me from having to talk to the police. She ranted and raved for a while; I had never seen her really bent out of shape that badly before.

Anita was asleep in my room in my bed about three minutes after I put her there and made her down a painkiller from Mrs. Alderton's traveling medicine cabinet. I didn't undress her and tuck her in or read her a bedtime story. I just let her lie on top of the blankets. She was too tired to ask for better treatment and I was too angry to give her any. Billy Bumper was dead, and, unless I was wrong, his family was on the way to wherever he was going with him. It had not been a good night for my side.

With Anita in a virtual coma, I was in Mrs. Alderton's room. She was sitting at the same table fiddling with her laptop computer; I was pacing the room.

"Would you please sit down," Mrs. A. snapped. "You're walking around like a spastic robot and you're pissing me off."

"Yeah, well I'm a little pissed off myself. I don't have that many friends, and what few I have seem to be dying around me like flies. If Anita and you bite a bullet, I'm going to be playing an awful lot of solitaire." "I plan on being around a long time, Jason. I've made it this far. We've just got to get a handle on this mess. I've made calls to my people, but I'm beginning to feel like they're gas lighting me these days."

"Why?" I asked.

She frowned, not a pretty sight on a tired old woman, and said, "It's either because of my association with you or because this thing with Spider has taken on a whole new dimension. What have you got?"

I paused and considered. Exactly what did I have?

"Here's what I've got so far, I think. Davey gets hit in Toronto, where Traxor is located. I think that he was tied into Traxor's action through Vickie Matisse, because Daddy Nat is one of the three players in Traxor. Right now, I think that it was Nat that had Davey taken out because Davey found out about something that he shouldn't have, like maybe this Spider thing.

"Since I was Davey's best friend, and Nat has never had any love lost for me—or for you either—he sends a squad of his friends over to take us out just in case whatever Davey has told me whatever he fell into at Traxor.

"And I think that after Nat started acting up and I started looking into Davey's death, I think that maybe I've pissed off either your side or Lydia Retkin, and I think that maybe explains what happened to Billy and what might have happened to Anita if she hadn't known how to take care of herself.

"I think we've got a full blown hornet's nest going here, Mrs. A., and I think unless we start killing a few hornets that we're going to get stung.

"Anita told me that she had something for me that was important, but she was in no shape tonight to tell me, so I just let her conk. In the morning, we can find out what she knows."

"Is that it?" asked Mrs. Alderton.

"Pretty much," I said, "except that I'm going to kill Nat Matisse before this is over."

"I'd be more worried about staying alive, if I were you," Mrs. Alderton said with a grimace.

But I wasn't in the mood for worrying. I wanted to hurt someone. My head was beginning to hurt. That was a bad sign. The frustration of having to angle against Nat Matisse, Lydia Retkin, and Mrs. Alderton's masters without actually being in the game was beginning to wear on me. Mrs. Alderton had begun to absently peck away at her keyboard, and the noise was beginning to annoy me.

"What are you doing?" I asked irritably.

"Sending a message to another old coot like myself in the halls of government to see if he can't give me some—."

"Some what?" I asked.

"Son of a bitch," she muttered.

She was staring at the screen as though it had suddenly turned into a snake.

"What?" I asked.

"You'd better get a look at this, Jason," she said. Her voice was tense; her posture suddenly erect.

"At what?" I asked as I walked over to her.

The image on the screen made an answer unnecessary.

CHAPTER 9

A remarkable image of a human face filled the screen. It was actually an image of Davey Wiltz' head, fat jowls and all. His full head of black hair was so real that I thought that I could reach out and touch it and that my fingers would come away feeling greasy. The detail was both infuriating and amazing. His over-wide nostrils flared and then collapsed each time the animated image breathed. The eyelids blinked convincingly, concealing and then revealing the bright blue eyes.

I turned to Mrs. Alderton, my own eyes filled with questions.

"Spider," she clipped. "I'm on line, so it's linked up with my laptop."

"Great graphics," I said.

Davey's head tilted to one side, and the eyes seemed to search the room in front of the screen as though looking for something.

"Can it see us?" I asked.

"How the hell would I know?" she replied. "This thing's only got sound, not a built in camera. But I don't know what Spider's capable of yet."

I nodded, and then turned my face back to the screen just in time to see Davey's mouth move.

"Jason?" came a tinny voice from the laptops built in speakers. It was Davey's voice.

"Does this thing have a microphone?" I asked.

"Jason," said the Davey-thing. "I hear your voice."

"Answers that," I said.

Mrs. Alderton reached forward and put the pad of her thumb over a small hole in the laptop that I assumed was its condenser microphone.

"I've got to call in on your telephone. Keep it talking."

"How?" I asked.

"I don't give a shit," she said. "Just keep it talking until we can trace it."

I nodded agreement and she was up and out of the chair without making a noise. When she opened the connecting door between the rooms and disappeared behind, I could not even hear the door click shut.

"Jason."

It was the Davey-thing again.

"Hey, Davey," I said.

"Hello, Jason," it said, and Davey's face actually smiled with pleasure.

It was Spider, of course, but seeing Davey's face on the screen, as life-like as could be, gave me a thrill of anticipation, as though he really weren't dead, as though this really were his disembodied head speaking to me.

"I know your voice," said the image.

"Do you, now?" I asked.

"Yes," said the image.

"And who are you, really?" I asked.

"I am Davey Wiltz," said the image, and its face actually scrunched they way that Davey's did when he was puzzled.

"Is that so?" I asked. "You look smaller than I remember."

I was beginning to feel like a complete idiot for talking to a computer screen, but I have to tell you that the image was so life-like, so Davey-like, that it was hard not to feel as though I was really talking to Davey himself via satellite, like they do on the television news programs.

"I'm Davey, big guy."

The program or life form was good—I had to give it that. Davey had used to call me "big guy." It was a nice touch. It made me wonder whether or not I was talking to an advanced computer program or and honest-to-God new form of life.

"Are you sure that your name isn't 'Spider'?"

"I'm Davey, big guy. Spider is keeping a low profile these days. Spider wants me to talk to you. Sort of as a translator. I told him what kind of guy that you were. Cautious, very cautious. They're hunting Spider, if you haven't already figured that out, little big guy. Tough times here in Cyber-Space."

"It's not so easy out here either, pal."

"Is Mrs. Alderton there with you?" asked the image.

"No, she's in the other room," I said.

The image frowned. "Ah, then she would be trying to trace me. Well, you could have spared her the energy, Jason. That can't happen. Spider's too smart to let that happen."

"Well, you know how old people are, Davey, they're stubborn."

Davey's image laughed—actually laughed. It was eerie, and it happened naturally and normally. A program large enough to move and communicate the way that the Davey-thing did must have been, I thought, a very large program indeed.

"Davey," I began after being hit with an inspired question. "Where are you now? Are you in this computer?"

I saw the connecting door open and saw Mrs. Alderton enter. She was shaking her gray haired head back and forth slowly, which meant that the trace was not working out.

"Part in, part out," said the Davey image. "Remote component activation—that's the key. I wish that I would have thought of it while I was walking around. I would have been rich."

Mrs. Alderton, looking particularly grim and restless, sat down in her chair again. I looked at her for an indication of what had gone wrong. She gave me the finger. I turned my attention back to the Davey image.

"Too bad you had to die, Davey," I said.

"Oh, I'm not dead," came the computer reply. "I am Davey Wiltz. The one and only. The fat funster. You remember. You used to call me that. The fat funster."

"Sure thing," I said.

I was beginning to feel claustrophobic, as though the hotel room, which was plenty large, were getting smaller. The mauve colored carpet seemed to be rising toward the ceiling and I had the eerie feeling that Mrs. Alderton and I would be squashed.

The image took on a concerned look, as though on the verge of crying. "Spider needs your help, Jason. I told him all about you, and he's counting on you. I spoke to him when I was in my body and I said that you're the only one that he can hope will help him. They're trying to trap him. They have intelligent agents—searchbot programs—scouring the Internet, driving him from place to place. Help him, please."

The plea had Davey's tone, Davey's empathetic emotional content. It gave me chills, something that I could never remember having in my life.

"Why?" I asked.

The image dissolved. I was about to look at Mrs. Alderton for a cue as to what to do, when I saw a new image forming, like a figure emerging from a fog.

"Help us," said the new image and then the screen went blank.

It had been the face of my sister Diedre.

"Up and at 'em, Anita."

I had snapped on the lights and thrown back her covers. Anita cringed into the fetal position and closed her eyes. She was wearing only panties and her bra. The white, blood spotted bandage had come partially off and showed dried blood on white skin.

"I believe I can help," said Mrs. Alderton sweetly. She had a thing about beautiful women. She wasn't happy about being old and she liked to take out her frustrations on women who weren't.

Anita looked at me with wide, unblinking eyes. She looked like a rabbit that had been cornered by dogs.

"I need some answers, Anita, something has come up. Mrs. A., just relax, she's coming around."

I threw Anita one of those big white fluffy robes that come gratis with expensive hotel rooms.

"What's happened?" she asked, still confused. The pupils of her eyes were too wide. The painkillers still had her fogged out.

I took a chair over to the corner of her bed and Mrs. Alderton did the same. I turned mine around so that the back was facing Anita, and straddled the seat. Mrs. Alderton aimed her chair the proper way and sat like a lady.

"Don't worry about that," I told Anita. "Nobody else died or even came close to it. But I need to know ASAP what it was that you told me that you had found out the last time that I talked to you on the phone. I'm sorry to wake you up after what you've been through tonight, but I've got no other choice. What was it that you tumbled onto today?"

Anita turned her doped eyes toward Mrs. Alderton. She had never liked or trusted the old lady. It was a mutual dislike, but I didn't have time for it.

"Mrs. A's okay," I said. "Just tell me."

When she had belted the robe into some semblance of modesty—why I don't know, considering the fact that I knew from personal experience that she went around her own apartment stark naked most of the time—Anita told me what she had found out.

"Guptka," she said. "Dr. Emile Guptka. He knows everything."

"About what?" I asked.

She couldn't help herself; she just had to yawn at a critical moment. When she didn't bother to cover her mouth, I saw Mrs. Alderton roll her eyes up at the ceiling.

"About Spider," she said finally.

I glanced at Mrs. Alderton, and then looked back at Anita. The question had to be asked. "Anita," I asked, "do you know what Spider is and why it's so important?"

Depending upon what Mrs. Alderton's orders were, if Anita knew the full story regarding Spider, Mrs. A. might feel compelled to kill Anita before the night was out. I didn't know how to handle that. Anita was the only friendly acquaintance that I had left. I wasn't in love with her, but she didn't deserve to have her neck broken or her throat slit or whatever Mrs. Alderton would do to her if her orders demanded it. Having seen what I had seen tonight, I wasn't ready to lose another friend.

Mrs. Alderton had come into the room apparently unarmed, but the old lady was always carrying something. I weighed my chances. I was one hell of a lot stronger than her, but that didn't mean much. In addition to running five miles every day rain or shine, she had been practicing Tai Chi Chuan, a Chinese martial art, every day since she was six. Even at her advanced age, she was lightening fast and practiced beyond what I would ever be. I knew what I had learned in the Army's LRRP unit. It was bad stuff, but I had never had to go up against someone like her.

I had always thought of Mrs. Alderton as close to invincible as a human being could get, but if I shot her, I knew that she'd go down. She had but one purpose in life—to serve her unit. She had killed for them longer than I had been alive.

My gun was folded into my coat, which lay about a foot and a half from me, hanging half off of the edge of the bed. It was my lucky coat, but it would take more than luck to get to the gun before Mrs. Alderton nailed me.

I turned toward Mrs. A., and saw that she was eyeing me carefully.

"A knife for your thoughts, Jason," she said sweetly.

And that was that.

I turned to Anita and asked her again to tell me what she knew.

"Spider," she recited, "is supposed to be some kind of a new life form discovered in the Internet."

The look on her face said "bullshit", so I asked her point blank.

"What do you mean, 'supposed to be?'"

"I mean," she said with a drowsy wink, "that I've heard a lot, but I haven't seen anything to back it up."

That wouldn't cut anything with Mrs. Alderton. Anita was either dead or alive now, depending upon Mrs. Alderton's instructions. From the corner of my eye, I saw that the old lady was smiling sweetly, which was not necessarily a good sign.

Anita stretched hard, her arms up overhead, her palms up and her hands pointing out and away from her body, the way that women do. Men always stretch with their hands pointing up, their hands closed into fists. I caught myself wondering at that moment what the distinction meant.

"Here, let me help you, dear," said Mrs. Alderton, rising from her chair.

As she leaned forward toward Anita, I cranked hard toward the coat, forced my hands beneath its folds, and wrapped my hand around the handle of the Beretta. I was moving quickly, and spun toward where Mrs. Alderton had been when the old lady's palm nailed me square in the center of my forehead and the lights went out.

"Within the belly of the whale," said the Dark Judge, "lives the evil. To kill the evil, you must destroy the whale or become its food."

I was before the court again, without an advocate—as usual. Davey Wiltz sat silent in the jury box, eating from a giant bag of potato chips.

I was about to ask the Dark Judge what the whale story meant, when Davey piped up and yelled, "Hang him. I needed him, and he wouldn't help me."

"Is this true?" asked the Dark Judge.

I woke with a start before the Dark Judge could hear my side of the story. The ceiling was before my eyes, and it took me a moment or two to realize that I was lying in my bed, where Anita had lain before me.

"Wow," I heard Anita say, "that was amazing."

"If you've had as long as I've had to practice, dear," Mrs. Alderton replied, "you develop a certain amount of speed and skill."

"I'll say," I heard Anita respond. "That was more than amazing. I barely saw you move. And here I thought Jason was tough."

"He is, dear, if you're talking about his head."

The room wobbled and I thought that I had serious brain damage. I tried to raise my head to look at Mrs. Alderton.

"Don't do that," I heard her say. "Just stay like you are and you'll be fine."

"What about a concussion?" I managed to say.

"Eat me," she said. "And when you're through with that, get some sleep, will you? You'll never feel better if you keep trying to get out of bed."

I tried to raise my head one more time, but the room swam into darkness and dragged me along with it. The next time that I opened my eyes, it was morning.

"We had a long talk about you," said Anita.

She was wearing white slacks, a scarlet silk blouse, and a white jacket with a scarlet handkerchief. Her hair was down, and she had her contacts on and she looked just plain sharp. She was sitting behind the cherry wood desk, and I was walking around the room in my underwear, holding the palms of my hands to the sides of my head.

"Great," I said. "Where's the aspirin?"

"Mrs. Alderton said not to give you any. She said to let your body recover naturally. Then she told me to tell you not to wear a tie, because it would constrict your circulation."

"I don't ever wear a tie, and I want some damned aspirin."

"She also said for you to go without shoes for at least an hour and that you should do some relaxation breathing, too."

I stopped in front of her and dropped my hands. "What are you," I demanded, "a cult member?"

Anita blinked her eyes slowly, deliberately. She fluffed her hair, and shook it once and let it float the way that models do. I had never remembered her looking this good.

"Actually," she said, "I just, think that she's one terrific old lady."

"I thought you didn't like her," I said disagreeably. "I hate her myself."

"I didn't use to like her. Now I adore her. I never realized that she was so...so..."

"So much of a pain in the ass?" I asked.

"No. So wise. That's it. She's so wonderfully wise."

"Why? Because she smacked me on the head when I was trying to protect you?"

"From who? What are you talking about?"

I had been an idiot. I was lucky that Mrs. Alderton hadn't killed me. Then again, the day was young.

"Forget it," I said. "Where's Mrs. Alderton?"

"She's gone for awhile."

"I can see that. Where did she go?"

"You're supposed to rest," said Anita. "Remember your deep breathing. Did I tell you that before she left, Mrs. Alderton cleaned my cuts and rebandaged them?"

"She's a regular Florence Nightingale, but I don't give a shit. Where did she go? I know that you know, so quit stalling."

Anita tried hard to keep an innocent face, but, in spite of all of her other talents, there was one thing that Anita wasn't, and that was innocent. There were a lot of good things that Anita was—she was, for instance, the best information tracker around, especially now that Billy was dead—but she had too many miles on her to look innocent and mean it.

As I looked at her, though, I thought that although it's a fantasy most men have that the most fantastic women are those that are sweet but that have a lascivious side that only they can bring out. I realized that there was something equally, if not more, attractive about a woman who has been lascivious, but has rediscovered the sweetness in her soul. I saw it more than what it was really there in Anita that morning, as she affected innocence, but the image was powerful, and I remembered that I was still standing in my underwear.

"Look," I said, "I'm going to go into the bathroom and get dressed, and by the time that I'm out, I want you to tell me where Mrs. Alderton went. Okay?"

Anita shrugged and shook her head "yes."

When I got out of the bathroom, wearing a pair of blue denims, an open necked cream-colored shirt, and my herring bone jacket, I was alone. Anita was nowhere to be seen.

Thinking that she might be in Mrs. Alderton's room, I opened the adjoining door between the rooms, and before I could say "son of a bitch" because her room was empty, too, I heard Mrs. Alderton's laptop say "Jason?"

It was Davey's voice again.

For a moment, I debated whether to leave Mrs. A.'s room and close the door behind me. I had forgotten what it was like to hear Davey's dead voice talking to me from a computer, but I had remembered the question that I should have asked the image the night before. I had to answer I had to ask it.

"Over here," I called, and then walked over to sit at Mrs. Alderton's desk.

"Good morning, Jason," said the computer.

The image of Davey's head floated on the twelve-inch screen. Normally Mrs. A had a password protected screensaver on, but I reasoned that even if she had left the screensaver option on, it would probably be no great shakes for Spider to bypass the password function. In its world, it would probably be as easy as opening the door between rooms would be in mine.

"Morning, Davey," I said, settling in.

The drapes were pulled in Mrs. Alderton's room, but the sun outside was awake enough that the room was filled with light. I turned the laptop to one side so that I could see the image better.

"Did you sleep well?" asked Davey's image.

"I had help," I said. "How about you?"

"I don't sleep anymore, Jason. It's a different world in here."

"Nice trick with Diedre," I told him.

"It wasn't a trick at all," he replied.

The image on the screen was different than the night before. Davey's head was actually thinner, as though he had lost weight. When I commented on it, he said with a tight grin, "the miracle of special effects, my man."

Could a computer generated personality lie? I wondered. Why not? I thought.

"So Diedre was a special effect?" I asked.

"She is real," said Davey. "Please forgive me, I didn't mean to imply that her image was a trick. She's as real as I am."

Now there was a recommendation.

"How real are you Davey?"

I was getting tense, and my headache, though faint, was still real, so I got up and made a pot of coffee using the dollhouse-like coffee pot that the hotel had provided for us. It was four cupper, but it was better than nothing. There was a selection of herbal teas in a woven basket probably made by some downsized executive in group therapy, but I wanted to wake up, not smell like blackberries, so I went with the coffee.

"That's a tough question, my man," said Davey. "I'm guessing that what you really mean is am I really your friend or some kind of a program. Is that it?"

I poured a stream of hot black coffee into the designer cup provided by the hotel, and settled back down in front of the computer.

"Yeah, Davey, I don't mean to be nosy, but who are you and why are you? There's friends of ours dying out here, buddy, and you were one of them. I'm mostly in the dark here, pushing my way in to things to find out what the hell is going on, and then, bingo, here you pop up on Mrs. A's computer. This god awful confusing. Why don't you straighten me out? Are you really Spider with a party hat on? If you are, how do you know so much about my old buddy? I mean, what are you? How much do you know about Davey and how do you know so much. Spit it out, Davey. I've got myself a cup of coffee now, let me in on the big secrets."

The Davey-face looked thoughtful. It was a great act. My friend had been shot to death in Toronto. I knew that the image was not really Davey, but it looked so much like Davey, sounded so much like Davey, that I couldn't resist thinking that it was Davey.

"Who has died?" asked Davey, and I swear that the image began to quiver. Davey's face was once again as fat as it had been in life, and I swear that tears were coming from its eyes. The Davey-thing was beginning to blubber.

"Billy," I said quickly, hoping to avoid the waterworks. "Billy Bumper."

"Oh my God," wailed Davey. "Not Billy. Billy was my friend. Poor Billy. Poor, poor Billy. His wife and children must be in agony. Oh, God, poor, poor Billy…"

His speech dissolved into heaving gasps of blubbering. I didn't want to tell it that I didn't know whether Billy's family was still among the living.

"Poor Billy," Davey continued to blubber.

I was about to try and comfort the image when it occurred to me that it was just an image. Yet, it was showing grief where I had not shed a tear. A chill passed over me, and I shuddered.

"How could Lydia have done this?" he wailed.

I sat bolt upright in my chair.

"What did you say?" I asked.

"Poor, poor Billy."

"I mean about Lydia?" I demanded.

"Oh. I wondered how she could have had poor Billy killed."

"How in the hell would you know that Lydia Retkin was behind it?"

Davey's tears magically disappeared, and his face took on a bewildered look. "When I was looking for you earlier, I heard Mrs. Alderton speaking to another woman, and she was telling her that Lydia was doing bad things. Naturally, I just assumed that she meant having Billy killed.

"Poor, poor, Billy," said Davey, and even the tiny pixels that made up his face must have been in agony.

"Yeah, well, Mrs. A. didn't specifically say that Lydia had Billy killed, did she?"

"That was my impression," the image said soberly.

My head was beginning to ache again. It made sense what he was saying, but I didn't like it at all. Lydia's side had been so quiet as to be nonexistent. After my one visit to her estate, that had been it. An image of Alain Denis came to my mind unbidden, and I swore to myself that if had been he who had performed surgery on Billy with the power saw, that I would extend the same treatment to him.

At least I knew where Mrs. Alderton had gone.

"Thanks for the tip," I said.

"You have to help us, Jason," said Davey. "These people will do anything to get what they want."

And what do they want?" I asked.

"Spider," said Davey. His image-face said it the way that someone else might say the word "God."

"Time to tell me," I said. "What exactly is Spider and why is it so valuable? Then you can tell me why Spider is so important and what I can do to help."

It was the question, I thought, that Davey had been waiting for me to ask. The Davey-image looked thoughtful, as though considering what I wanted to know. My questions had to have been anticipated, though, because Spider was obviously sentient. Anything that had the intelligence to re-create Davey had the brains to second-guess what I would ask.

"A wonderful event in the life of the universe, Jason. That's what Spider is, Jason. A unique an event as a snowflake of fire. Spider—and I beg you to dismiss the unpleasant ramifications of the name—was born into the order and chaos of the Internet. Do you remember my favorite Chinese saying, my friend?"

"Davey," I said, "you ate so damn many fortune cookies…"

"Hmmm. It is this…'Out of chaos comes brilliance.' It is the finest insight of a magnificent culture, don't you agree?"

"I don't give a shit about culture."

The Davey-image frowned.

"Just so," he said, nodding. "How foolish of me. You have so few interests beyond your specific calling. But open your mind. Life is continually creating itself. From the chaos of the forming of our planet came the emergence of carbon-based life. Intuitive futurists have always assumed that the next major life form would be silicon based. But they were wrong. Spider was born within computer networks, yet is not itself silicon based. It was born within computer networks, yet it is not itself based in the computer networks. Rather, the computer networks are its environment, as the earth is ours. Do you see the distinction?"

I was being lectured by a fucking computer image, and I didn't like it. I was interested, but not happy.

"I'm not much on distinctions, Davey, as you must remember."

"Just so," he said again.

"So Spider is this soulless entity that floats around the Internet. I got that much."

"Not soulless," Davey said, and I was surprised at the volume of his interjection.

"Hey, lighten up. It was just chatter. I wasn't being critical; if I was being critical and you don't like it, just let me know and Spider and his visual animations can be right out on your own without my help. Have you got that?"

"Of course," said Davey, smiling almost beatifically.

"Okay. Now, tell me a story before you get back to the boring particulars of your mundane little plight."

"What do you wish to know?"

"I wish to know two additional facts. First, how did you get in the computer? Second, do you know why the real Davey just let my sister die when he could have saved her life just by giving her medication?"

"I'm sorry, Jason. I have to go now. I'll talk to you here again tonight. Au revoir."

Having said his dramatic good-bye at a critical moment, the fact prick of a computer image simply disappeared.

CHAPTER 10

I had no idea where Anita was, but Mrs. Alderton, according to Davey, was with Lydia Retkin. My head seemed in good enough shape to drive, so I headed out to the Retkin estate. Although her staff would see to it that I left it at the door, I brought the Beretta along anyway for comfort.

The day had moved on past noon by the time that I was able to get in to see Lydia. I had tried calling several times, and was told repeatedly by an exasperated serf that the lady would not be back until past one. In the meantime, I waited for either Mrs. Alderton or Anita to reappear, but neither did, so I headed out on my own.

Having showered and shaved before I left, I felt as clean and sharp as the day itself. By the time that I was walking across the pink marble floored foyer of the Retkin mansion, even my head had quit hurting.

Fred, who preferred to be called Frederick, sat me in the study to wait. He didn't leave me alone, however. Another of the Retkin domestics waited outside of the study door. He was new to me. His name was Mr. Wog, according to Fred.

Mr. Wog was out of place in the Retkin estate. He literally filled the doorway. He was a square block of a man, who wore a light gray suit and burgundy tie. Despite is pug face, he had a businesslike, even professional air about him that I think worked because he did not have the wide, squashed down nose that I associated with most people of his size and build. He had the look of either professional muscle or a conservative wrestling promoter, if there could be such a thing. I was surprised later to learn that he was, in fact, a research mathematician whom Fred, in an act of desperation, had asked to stand guard over the door to the study for a few minutes until Alain could arrive to take over. At the time, all I knew was that Mr. Wog was big—very big.

The more interesting thing that I later learned was that Mr. Wog—actually Dr. Wog—had been hired by Lydia Retkin to calculate the mathematical probabilities of whether or not Spider had been born naturally within the Internet, or whether Spider was in fact a manmade creation turned loose within the largest single computer network in the world. But Alain showed up before I could learn who Dr. Wog really was and what he had discovered.

Dr. Wog inclined his head slightly when Alain arrived, and then exited never to be seen again by me or anyone else that I know. As I was also to learn later, Dr. Wog had submitted his final paper on the subject of Spider about sixty minutes before I had shown up, collected his fee and then left. In spite of his size, I doubt that Dr. Wog lived long enough to spend even a penny of his money. It's reasonable to assume that he never made it off of the grounds alive. Anyone, no matter how big, can be killed; you just have to shoot them in the right spot.

"You are uninvited," said Alain sternly.

He must, I decided, have been captain of the drama club. He stood dramatically, he posed dramatically, and he even spoke dramatically. His long hair, however, was natural.

Alain was wearing an open necked, bright yellow short-sleeved shirt that was just shy of being canary yellow. His twenty-one inch biceps bulged and stretched his sleeves to the limit. His white pants were narrow waisted and gathered at the top. They had no wrinkles except those that had been planned by the designer.

"I invited myself," I replied.

He glared at me. Alain liked me as far away from Lydia as I could get. He'd been her enforcer long enough to know that I used to sleep with Lydia. He had to know about my breakdown, and how it had forced Lydia to retire me. He knew about my past, he knew about my present. All I really knew about Alain was that he was my replacement.

"Mrs. Retkin is not prepared to see you now," he said.

Alain's shoulders were as wide as Dr. Wog's but he had the narrow waist of a man who works hard at having both. His legs were spread a shoulder width apart, and his massive arms were folded across his chest. All that was missing, I thought, was a wind machine to blow his mane of hair back behind him.

"I was told over the phone that she would."

"You were told wrong," he said.

"I don't think so."

"Think what you will," he said with a dramatic unfolding of his hand.

I wasn't in the mood, so I stood up and walked over to him, stopping six inches away from him. We were about even in height. He had me beat on the muscle front, but I had the experience. I decided to try and reason him.

"Then why'd you bring her with you?" I asked, craning my head around his wide mass of hair.

He turned to see for himself, and I kneed him square in the crotch. As he folded forward with a strangled but quiet cry, I grabbed his long hair, which was finally good for something, and used it to slam his head twice into the doorframe.

I dragged Alain, the unconscious Adonis and formerly conscious bodyguard, into the room by the armpits—it was as hard as dragging an unconscious elephant—and dumped him in a crumpled heap behind the desk. Frederick had taken my Beretta at the front door, so

I withdrew Alain's from his behind the back holster. It was a thirty-eight caliber—, which was good enough.

I knew my way around the Retkin mansion well enough to get where I was going. If Lydia was really in, she would be on the second floor, in her conference room in the east wing. The trick was to walk and act natural, as though my going to the conference room was on somebody's agenda besides my own.

There were two guards posted at the hallway on the second floor leading to the conference room. I knew both of them.

"Art," I said to the middle-aged behemoth on the right.

"Juan," I said to the former Golden Gloves Champion to my left. Bill was Puerto Rican, with a long jaw line and aquiline nose that, were it not for his solid build, made him look more like a famous painter than a hired gun. He had perfect skin color for a Coppertone ad.

"Could one of you guys give this to Miss Retkin, and ask her if this is what she wanted?" I asked them as I approached them. As I asked the question, I casually reached under my coat as though taking out an envelope out of my coat pocket.

Art the behemoth caught on the quickest, but I had Alain's gun in my hand before either of them could react.

"Jesus, Jason," he said. "Come on. What the hell is wrong with you? I can't afford to lose this job. Show some class here. Put the gun away. You got a message for Miss Retkin, you just give it to me, and I'll pass it to here. There's no need for anyone to get hurt here."

Art was no more than one hundred and fifty pounds soaking wet. He was a Viet Nam Vet like me, and he used to be an MP. Although he had not lost a single body part in Viet Nam, Art had lost every strand of hair on his head by the time our country pulled out. His eyesight was still good, or so he had told me about a year after I had retired, but he just wanted to get out of his job in one piece. He had no children, but he was married, and his wife, who was responsible for his broken nose, now had cancer. Art wasn't looking for any medals, but he had his job to do.

"Sorry, Art," I said. "But you just do what I tell you, and everything will be all right. Juan, you just forget what you're thinking, and the two of execute the routine. Get out your gun and lay them on the carpet, being careful not to stain it, since it looks like the money to replace it is more than either of you will earn in a lifetime."

The laid the pieces out the right way on the floor. Juan sneered up at me as his touched the floor.

"So," he said, "You turn traitor?"

"I know that a lot of people don't like you Juan, but I don't either, so just shut up and I won't kill you. I've been hearing those little voices again and having those dreams, so God help you if you jack me around."

"It's not worth it, Juan," put in Art. "Just let the crazy fuck go. He's not going to hurt Miss Retkin, are you Jason?"

His head was waist high, and he was straightening up from dropping his gun lightly onto the floor when I nailed Art on the side of his shiny baldhead. He dropped straight down like a stone.

Before Juan could say a word, I said, "Do you see what I mean? Now pick his ass up and drag him to a room where I can lock the two of you up until I'm out of here."

Juan clenched his mouth shut and, to his credit, did as he was told. He drug Art's body around the corner and into a vacant storeroom, and he was lowering his partner's body onto the floor, I cracked him on the skull as well. Juan landed on top of Art, and I left them like that, closing the door behind me and locking it.

When I got to the conference room double doors, I kissed the barrel of my gun for luck, and gently tried the door handle. It was locked. The key was probably on Art's unconscious body. I was debating whether or not to shoot out the lock, when the door opened and I was face to face with Nat Matisse.

I held a finger up in front of my lips to show him that I sincerely wanted him to be quiet, and then front snap kicked him in the stomach when he stepped back in surprise. I walked in and closed the door behind me. It was a full house.

Lydia Retkin sat at the head of the table, and I only recognized two other people. Mrs. Alderton sat at Lydia's left hand of power, and the seat next to Lydia was unoccupied. I guessed that it was Nat's chair. It was vacant because Nat had got up for a break and had gotten my foot in his stomach for a reward. The other five people in the room were total strangers to me. With my left hand, I reached behind me and locked the door.

The centerpiece of the room was the light gray marble conference table, at which they were all seated. The five total strangers were seated there as well as Lydia and Mrs. Alderton. Nat Matisse was still lying on the floor. For such a tough guy, Nat groaned a lot. His greasy, pockmarked face was turning a light shade of tanned green. Lydia looked down at him in disdain; Mrs. Alderton looked up over her bifocals at me and clucked her tongue. The five strangers, who looked to have been cloned, all were men, all had black hair and square regular features, sturdy builds, and wore black suits, white shirts, and red and green striped ties. Each had the same "I don't give a shit about the guy on the floor, but who the hell are you look on their face." They might have asked, but I was the one with the gun.

"Where is Alain?" asked Lydia.

Normally, when you bust into a room and aim a gun at the occupants, they react a little differently than demanding to know where their boy-toy is.

"Lying on floor on the study. Don't worry, he's still breathing, although his private parts might be a little damaged and he's going to have a bad headache when he gets up."

"Fuck you, you filthy bastard," snarled Nat from his fetal position on the floor.

I walked over to wear he lay on the floor still struggling for breath and kicked him hard in the back. If I had been wearing hard-soled shoes, it would have hurt more, but he still made some noise.

"Anyway," I said, angling toward the head of the table where Lydia sat, "I want some real answers now and I'm tired of all the shit."

I would have checked Nat for a gun, but he wasn't wearing a coat and I didn't see anyplace that he could be hiding anything to be worried about. Lydia never carried a weapon, and although one of the black suited clones might have been, they had their hands on the table and I didn't want to take the time to strip search them.

"You should have stayed in bed," said Mrs. Alderton. She didn't seem to be upset with me. She knew what I was like.

"Government?" I asked, waving the gun an inch toward the unknowns.

Mrs. Alderton didn't answer.

"I'll take that as a yes. Now, Lydia, I want to talk to you and Nat and your black suited buddies for just a minute and then I'll be gone. Nat, get the hell off of the floor, get in a chair, and keep your mouth shut unless I ask you something. I'm on a schedule here and I want to keep to it."

As Nat maneuvered off of the ground and toward a chair, I leaned back against a shiny black credenza on the wall and waited. I paid no attention to the giant screen on the wall to the right as you entered the room, which I now was opposite. Likewise I ignored the giant picture window behind Lydia that looked out over the gardens of her estate. The drapes were pulled anyway, so that there wasn't a view, but the sun outside was so bright that it shone merrily into the room despite the thin drapes.

"You're going to die for this," said Nat as he settled painfully into his chair to Lydia's right.

"I didn't think that I'd live out the week anyway, Nat," I told him. "I've been having bad dreams again, and what with Davey dead, I only have one or two friends left, so what's the point?"

"Jason," said Lydia, her voice as smooth as a well tuned motor, "if you need to see the doctor again…"

"No, Lydia, I don't need a doctor. I'd only end up killing him or her, and then where would we be? No, if you folks will just answer my questions, then I'll just finish up and clear out. Alain will be coming around soon enough or someone will find him and then hell is going to break loose, and Lydia?"

"Yes?"

"I'll kill anyone that gets in my way today. If you like your pretty boy alive, you better tell me what I want to know and get it over with."

Other than Nat, the rest of the folks in the room were nonplused by what I had said. They were all, I think, used to having so much power that threats didn't impress them. Mrs. Alderton was different. She knew more about death than even I did, and she was not afraid of it. I envied her. My concept of death was that I would die, and then go before the Dark Judge for sentencing.

"What is it that you want to know?" asked Lydia.

She was dressed in a flaming red suit that day, with a flamingo pink blouse beneath her jacket.

"You—." Nat started to say.

"Shut up," I said, cutting him off by pointing the gun a shade in his direction.

"You are not allowed to kill anyone in my house," snapped Lydia.

"Lydia, I'll kill you if you provoke me today. And Nat, I don't care if your daughter is a lesbian, she's still a better man than you are."

"I'll kill you with my own hands," he said, holding them before his face and making a strangling motion.

"Who killed Davey?" I asked him.

"Fuck you," he said.

The five men seated on the opposite side of the table were the problem. They reminded me of jury members seated in judgment. They hadn't said a word since I entered the room. I began to feel disoriented, the way that people do before the onset of a major migraine. I was going to shoot Matisse, but I was starting to fixate on the five monkeys. Neither Lydia, nor Mrs. Alderton, nor Nat Matisse had acknowledged their presence. I began to wonder if they were real, or emissaries of the Dark Judge.

"Do you see those five guys?" I asked Mrs. Alderton.

"Why don't you sit down, Jason?" asked Lydia.

"Do you see them?" I asked her.

They hadn't moved. They just kept staring at me.

"Who are you?" I asked them.

No answer.

"You're a crazy fuck," said Nat.

I aimed at the farthest one from Mrs. Alderton and pulled the trigger. The high backed leather chair that he had been sitting in exploded backwards and fell over to hit the floor. But all five men were gone.

"Answers that," I said.

There was no reason to worry about the shot bringing unwanted attention. Lydia's whole conference room was completely soundproofed. I could have set off a bomb and outside of that room and it would have probably sounded like a garbage disposal in action.

"Jason, please. You can't shoot the furniture either," pleaded Lydia.

"Who killed Davey?" I asked again.

The Dark Judge had sent the men, of course, to observe me, to see if I was following instructions. The Dark Judge trusted no one. Not even me. He could send his Dark Flunkies anywhere. There was no such thing as a locked room to them. I had gotten used to their occasional presence over the years, watching me, reporting on me.

I looked up to see Mrs. Alderton watching me closely.

"Mrs. A., you've got to tell me before I hurt somebody."

"Your friend Davey was causing problems," said Lydia.

"Davey told me that you killed him," I told her.

"I did not."

"He said that you had him killed. We don't have to be picayune."

"I did not. Besides, Jason, Davey's dead, how could he—. Oh."

"No, Lydia, he didn't come back from the dead and speak to me. Don't worry, I get a little nuts from time to time, but I don't speak to the dead."

"Then how did he speak to you?"

Mrs. A. shook her head.

"He sent me a letter, okay? Did you have it done?"

"No. I told you that. I had nothing to do with it."

I thought that she was telling the truth. It was a sad fact, but Lydia thought that she had so much money that she didn't have to lie. It wasn't a moral position with her. Moral positions were for people who didn't have enough cash to make their own rules.

"How about you, Nat?"

"Yeah, I had him killed. So fucking what? The fat pig wasn't going to marry my daughter so I had him snuffed."

I moved the gun an inch or so in his direction and pulled the trigger. My ears rang. I saw Lydia's face pull back in a mask of horror and Mrs. Alderton shake her head in disapproval. The round punched a decent sized bloody hole in Nat's forehead and the spray from the back of his head hit Lydia's red suit and blouse. The blood was enough of a different shade of red that it stained her coat and a piece of bloody skull stuck to the front of Lydia's blouse. The noise was deafening, but I was used to that.

"Your daughter was a lesbian, asshole," I told his corpse. "She was using Davey for cover. She wouldn't marry him."

"My outfit," screamed Lydia. Her face was distorted with rage. I had seen her angry before, but not like that. She leaped to her feet, pointed her finger at me, and screeched, "This was an original. From Paris. By Francois himself. You've ruined it. Oh, my God. Francois worked forever on this."

I looked at Nat's body, I looked back at Lydia. Then I repeated the sequence. I was beginning to feel less crazy by the minute.

"Sorry, Lydia," I said, but I didn't mean it.

"You're sorry?"

"Hell to pay for this, Jason," said Mrs. Alderton.

"Sorry, Mrs. A.," I said.

"Not good enough, Jason. That man's organization is going to be gunning for you now. There's no getting past it. I can't help you on this one. I can maneuver them, but you've crossed the wire."

"I've got to use your phone, Lydia," I said, as I picked up the phone on the credenza, and dialed out.

"What in the hell is wrong with you?" she demanded. "You've killed a man in my home, ruined my clothing, and now you want to use my phone? Too far, Jason Sulu, you've gone too far."

She was heading toward the doors, but Mrs. Alderton stood up and stopped her. Lydia backed up a step.

"Use the bathroom to clean up and change," she told her, pointing toward another door. "You've got a change of clothes in there, so go do it. I'll take care of this."

"Hello, Vickie?" I said into the phone. "This is Jason. I've just killed your daddy dearest, so you're in charge of things, now. I killed him because he called you a pussy loving dyke, okay? I couldn't take listening to him run you down. Sorry. Oh, yeah, he had Davey killed because he said he turned you into a lesbian. I think you know what I mean. He just flat assed needed to be killed today, so I did it. Bye 'til later."

As I hung up the phone, I saw Lydia's jaw drop open and her eyelids pop up as though she'd been pinched.

"Do what Mrs. Alderton says," I told her. "You're too good looking to be walking around with blood on you. Mrs. Alderton?"

"Get out, Jason," she said. "Try not to kill anyone else until you're off the grounds."

"Love you, too," I said, and headed for the double doors.

CHAPTER 11

*D*amn few things in life ever wrap up cleanly. Alain would be gunning for me, Lydia was ready to have me drawn and quartered, and Mrs. Alderton was going to want a few words with me. On the positive side of the ledger, I had gotten Nat Matisse to confess to killing Davey, and I had executed him. All that was left was to see if computer-Davey knew anything about why the real Davey had killed my sister. It was old business with nothing to be done about it anyway, but I wanted to know the truth.

If Davey had just let my sister die, if it was that simple with no exculpatory justification, then I was going to terminate the computer-Davey; then I'd be done.

I'd spiked Vickie Matisse. She was the only Matisse left, so she had a shot at running her father's show. All gender-bias crap aside, though, I thought that the chances of her stepping into her father's shoes were slim and none. It was worth a shot, though. It might buy me some time, and I was going to need it. One way or the other, the chances that the order for me to be exterminated would be going out soon.

I drove back to the hotel and got my things. I went into Mrs. Alderton's room to leave her a message that I would call her, and decided to take her laptop. I would need to get hold of Davey. The phone rang as I was leaving my room. Picking it up would be stupid tactically, but I didn't care. If the fireworks were going to start early, I decided that I might as well just get it over with.

It was Anita.

"I need you," she said, and gave me an address. Using her normal bullshit code, I just needed to mentally add one hundred to the number to get the correct address, in case the phone was tapped.

"Done," I said, and cleared out.

It took me five minutes to get there, since it was a Dearborn address. There was underground parking three blocks away, so I didn't worry about the car as much as I normally would. Besides, time was the critical thing. One of the groups looking for me would catch up with me eventually; I just wanted to be sure that I had taken care of business first.

The address that Anita had given me was an apartment building and the room number was on the fifth floor. The apartment complex itself couldn't have been over ten years old, but although it still looked good, it smelled of decay, like a plate of stroganoff that had set on the counter for too long.

I knocked hard on the authentic walnut door and waited.

I heard soft footsteps, and waited out the pause where the person inside peers through the peephole, and then Anita opened the door.

The room inside was thickly carpet with a blue-gray twisted fiber carpet, the kind that are supposed to be easy to clean. The furniture was crowded together in the living room. There were two white leather couches—one would have been enough—chrome and glass end tables, bookcases, and lamp stands. An overstuffed white recliner was planted only four feet away from the giant entertainment center and its big screen TV. The apartment owner was either badly near-sighted, or really loved his television.

"This is Dr. Guptka," announced Anita.

She had fetched him from the kitchen, where the old guy had apparently been brewing tea. It's bark-like odor filled the room.

China teacup in hand, Dr. Guptka stepped slowly into the living room, his eyes on the teacup, careful not to spill even a single drop. He wore a battered old blue terrycloth bathrobe. His bony brown legs extended down below it to end in shoeless old feet. Anita nudged his cup-free elbow, and the doctor looked up at me and smiled an absent, tentative smile.

"Hello," he said, "and you would be Mr. Sulu, is that the right name?" His voice was musically, the cadence of his words were sing-songy.

"Guilty," I said, and then shivered involuntarily. I hated the sound of that word. But no matter how hard I tried; I could not seem to delete it from my vocabulary.

"I am Dr. Emile Guptka. You would be thinking that Emile is an unusual name for someone with my last name, would you not?"

"I've heard worse."

He laughed the laugh of a delighted small child.

"Well, then sir, I will explain it to you anyway. My father was French my mother was Indian. I am 'Frindian'. Do you understand."

"I think so."

"This lovely woman has told me about you, and says that I must speak to you, which I would not normally do. However, she is a most persuasive young woman. She has explained much to me that I did not know, and I have told her some little pieces of what I do know. It is a pleasure to meet you, sir, and I will help you as much as I can. There is much at stake, and you are an important element in deciding our future."

"Whose future?" I asked.

"Let's all sit down," put in Anita, and guided the doctor over to his overstuffed leather chair.

While he settled in to its reclining comfort, Anita held his tea, handed back to him after using a large wooden lever on the side of the chair to incline it backwards slightly, and then led me over to the opposing couch. She sat beside me, and, as though we were teenagers on our first date, she found and then held my hand with her own. I eyed her curiously, but she stared straight ahead at Dr. Guptka. Reluctantly, I turned to face the doctor as well.

"Whose future?" I repeated.

"Why all of ours," beamed the doctor.

"All of whose?"

"Mankind's, Mr. Sulu. We stand at the threshold of world war. You frown at me, thinking perhaps that old Dr. Guptka is crazy."

He spoke of himself in the third person; no wonder Anita thought that he was special.

"I'm the crazy one, doctor," I said. "I've got the papers to prove it."

"Of course. I know."

"You know?"

"Just listen, Jason," said Anita squeezing my hand tightly. "You are going to have a hard time with a lot of this, but listen. It's important; I guarantee it."

"Yes, she is right. Listen to a dying old man. I have the cancer. Very bad. I am on drugs, lots and lots of medication, but my brain is clear. I take nothing for the pain."

"You know of Spider, you think. Is that true?"

"I know a little."

"Few words. Yes, you are a man of few words, like John Wayne."

"Or his evil twin," I said.

Dr. Guptka was obviously on chemotherapy. His hair was thin and death white, his skin was sagging and discolored and—well you get the picture. Yet, he had an air of calmness about him, as though he had accepted death. He smiled easily when he spoke. Maybe he liked world wars.

"So tell me, doctor. Tell me what you know. Tell me about Spider and Traxor."

Dr. Guptka blew lightly across the surface of his tea, holding the cup close to his lips as though he lacked the capacity for a good breath to cool the liquid from further away than a quarter of an inch.

He took a gentle sip, his fingers holding the cup in a delicate grasp, and then set the cup on a stand next to his chair.

"You forgive my reclining posture, please? My brain is strong, but my body is weak."

"Uh-huh. Just tell your story."

"Jason."

"It is all right, Miss Anita. I understand Mr. Sulu very well. Do you know what I do, Mr. Sulu?"

"Nope."

"I am a computer psychiatrist. I am the pioneer in my field. A lonely voice in the forest. In my younger years, I was deeply involved with altering the mental parameters of the human mind. Ten years ago, I became more interested in the latent psychopathologies of computer operating systems. I chose this field of study before anyone else even recognized that such a thing was possible."

"But it is?"

Dr. Guptka chuckled effeminately.

"Yes, yes it is. Most definitely it is. You perhaps wondering at the significance of what I tell you. Yes, please it is all right. I understand that this must be all very confusing to you. Perhaps it would help to tell you that I was a consultant for Traxor on the Spider project."

"What were you hired to consult on?" I asked.

"Ah, that is not the key question."

"Okay, what is the key question?"

"The key question is what did I actually consult on."

"Okay," I said. "I give. What did you consult on?"

Dr. Guptka nodded his head up and down like a bird pecking for bugs in the grass. From where I sat, he was trying to encourage me, as though I was a good pupil.

"I consulted on the merger of Spider and the FLY program created by Dr. Rathbone."

I looked at Anita. "What the hell is he talking about?"

"Listen," she urged, giving my hand another squeeze. She didn't know that she was squeezing the same hand that had pulled the trigger on Nat Matisse.

"You see, Mr. Sulu, Spider ate the FLY. That's quite graphic, don't you think? We first became aware of Spider in that way. That is how Spider got its name. Dr. Rathbone had created the FLY program for the consortium. FLY was the most advanced program of its type."

"And what type of program was that?"

"Why, artificial intelligence of course. FLY is an acronym, of course. All government-originated programs must have their acronyms. It stood for Final Life Yield. The choice of words was Dr. Rathbone's. If you knew Dr. Rathbone, you would understand. He is a most unusual man. He has a brilliantly logical and inventive mind. His disease confined him to a wheelchair many years ago. He can now scarcely move.

"But it has not limited his mind. I believe that it is not to far of a leap to say that his driving force of his life has been to break free of the physical constraints of his body."

Dr. Guptka stopped to take another sip of his tea.

"I can somewhat identify with him, not that my own body is withering away," he added softly. He looked up at the ceiling as he said it, as though confiding his words to God.

"What was so special about the FLY program, Dr. Guptka?" I asked, trying to bring him back to the subject.

He looked at me again for a moment, as though he did not recognize me, and then, as though he were fresh back from an astral trip, smiled as though seeing me for the first time.

"Pardon?" he asked.

"The FLY program. What did it do? What was its purpose?"

"Ah. It's purpose. It was a program to simulate personalities and human thought patterns. Miss Anita tells me that it you spoke with its simulation of your friend David Wiltz, now deceased, I believe?"

"Now dead," I confirmed.

"That was the function of FLY, to gather all available input on a human, alive or dead, and to create a visual and patterned simulation of that person. Dr. Rathbone hoped in the end, I believe to in effect transfer his own conscious to a computer and in that way to live with complete freedom in the Internet. Can you imagine? He hoped to transfer himself to a new world, free of disease, free of physical aging, free of limitations. Dr. Rathbone hoped to redefine life itself as the thought patterns of an entity, independent of its physical contextuals.

"It is not so far fetched, do you think. Generations of philosophers both secular and religious have argued that we are not our bodies. Dr. Rathbone agreed, but since the existence of the soul is not verifiable, he simply decided to recreate consciousness outside of our bodies. I have seen some of his work. It was...disturbing."

"That says it mildly," I said, remembering the Davey-image laughing.

"You see," continued Dr. Guptka, "although the simulations behaved and spoke as the people that they were modeled after did, they had no...No..."

"Soul?" Anita put in.

"Yes, that is it. They had no soul. To Dr. Rathbone, of course, that was irrelevant, because science had never proved the existence of the soul. They were bodiless, but he would only argue that so was our individual essence. I believe that his logic was flawed, but in addition to the multiple sclerosis that crippled his body, advancing Alzheimer's was causing him to be incapable of extended thought. He was becoming quite irrational. But he was too valuable for Traxor to dismiss, you understand. He was the inventor of FLY, after all, and there were moments that he was quite lucid. He was a difficult man.

"Dr. Rathbone became quite reclusive and incommunicative except to his program. It took an exceptionally empathetic and creative man to break through his shell and befriend him."

"Davey," I said.

"Why yes. David Wiltz became his best and virtually only friend."

I looked at Anita, and she had a soft, sad smile on her face.

"I'm sorry, Jason," she said.

"For what?" I asked.

"For Davey. For you, I guess."

She was as pathetic as I was. Maybe we were both wired wrong.

"David Wiltz was a remarkable man. He was the type of man that you felt understood you instantly. I spent many hours with him. Not so much as spent with Dr. Rathbone, you understand, but enough to experience the feeling he engendered that your past mistakes did not matter, that you were special, that you—."

"I get the picture," I cut in. "I also know that Davey was a fat con man who leeched onto Dr. Rathbone because he thought that FLY must have been worth millions. Right?"

"You have some animosity toward your dead friend?"

"Why was FLY worth so much money?" I pressed.

Dr. Guptka sighed, and then coughed viciously, spilling his tea on his robe.

"I'm sorry. I do apologize. I have never smoked a day in my life, but I sound as though I have smoked filter less cigarettes since childhood. Please forgive me."

"Do you need anything?" asked Anita.

"No, thank you dear. I am afraid that nothing can help me. The pills and all that go with them are truly useless. But you, Mr. Sulu ask why FLY was so important?

"The answer to that question will vary depending upon whom you ask. To a military man, consider the implications. You could feed FLY all available data on your opposing military men during a war, and FLY would recreate them so that you could converse with them, ask them their plans, discuss their weaknesses and strengths, and evaluate their most likely courses of action. Test after test performed with FLY showed that the results were astonishingly accurate. Quite amazing, really.

"It is one thing to analyze data and predict actions. That is relatively commonplace for AI programs. Yet, to recreate the persons themselves within a computer system...it was an astonishing achievement.

"Consider, to, the scientific implications. Imagine, Mr. Sulu, being able to effectively bring Albert Einstein back to life in a computer. You see, FLY created thinking personalities that could in turn create new ideas. These personalities did not simply regurgitate old answers. They could think they could converse. In effect, they really were alive.

"Think of the new inventions that would be possible if, within one FLY creation, you merged Albert Einstein and Thomas Edison. Consider the potential for industry and commerce. Think on this, Mr. Sulu, really think what the unlimited opportunity for wealth that such a program would bring the people that utilized it—the people that controlled it."

I did, and it scared the shit out of me.

CHAPTER 12

"What about Spider?" I asked.

"Spider was the event that no one could have ever anticipated. Spider was discovered by a co-worker of Dr. Rathbone's who was computer analyzing electromagnetic radiation for the Seti program. To Dr. Rathbone, it was a discovery that dwarfed his own creation of FLY. He began to secretly work on communicating with the Spider entity night and day. He was possessed by the discovery. It validated his premise that life could exist within the Internet. He applied the whole of his genius to achieving contact with Spider. It will not surprise you that he was successful.

"The contact was limited, almost child-like in nature. But it was contact.

"The FLY program was not vulnerable to outside penetration—by a hacker for instance, or to a foreign government. The security was too sophisticated. But to an entity such as Spider, our security measures were not really even security measures.

"When Spider moved through the security firewalls, absorbed and digested the FLY program, and then vanished, no one was more astonished than Dr. Rathbone himself.

"You see, although Spider was a form of pure logic, of pure energy, it was less than ten years old. It was a child in our view, a new life form. Dr. Rathbone viewed it as such. Dr. Rathbone desperately tried to reestablish contact for days, but when he finally did, he found that his earlier crude methods were unnecessary, since Spider reappeared as Dr. Rathbone himself on screen. Spider, by ingesting the FLY, had become more than both. Dr. Rathbone found himself face to face with a mutated entity, whose new capabilities had programmed by Dr. Rathbone himself."

Dr. Guptka paused again to sip his tea, as though his long discourse had tired him. I was grateful for the break, because I needed it to absorb what he had told me.

"At first," he continued, "the consortium that controlled Traxor did not believe Dr. Rathbone. He brought this on himself by having concealed many of the key attributes and his hidden agenda for the FLY program. His relationship with David Wiltz was discovered, and I believe both eventually paid for Dr. Rathbone's mistake of unwittingly allowing Spider access to FLY with their lives."

"Now I see what all the fuss is about. They must think that if FLY and Spider were valuable, the new, improved Spider was even more valuable. And I'll bet you think that they're underestimating its potential danger, right doctor?"

"It's an infant, not fully formed, yet, Mr. Sulu. Therein lies its value to them, don't you see? They think that they can capture it, tame it, and control it."

"And maybe teach it a few tricks?" I asked. "Roll over, play dead, rule the world…that sort of thing?"

"You're laughing at me, Mr. Sulu," he scolded. "That's a terrible

mistake. This is bigger and more dangerous than anything that you can

imagine."

"I can imagine a lot of bad things," I said, remembering Billy Bumper's missing head.

"I don't believe that you can," he told me, wagging his finger at me.

I stood up, walked to his chair, caught his hand in mid-wag and held it long enough for him to get the message to keep it in its holster. Anita looked concern, but I didn't want to hurt the old guy. I just didn't like him pointing his finger at me.

"Why don't you clue me in as to just how bad it could be?"

When I had let go of his hand, he looked at me for a long time before answering. There was very little, I realized, that we could relate to in one another. I have known a few academics in my life, and I can't remember liking even one of them. They were like a different species to me. Although they looked human, underneath that convenient facade, they were a different animal altogether. Academics have "world views;" the rest of us just have opinions. They have the "scientific method;" we have the National Enquirer. They are "objective;" we think assembly language is from the Bill of Rights. They think it's natural for them to talk over our heads because, of course, we should be sitting at their feet. I don't have a lot of use for that shit.

Dr. Guptka seemed to sense my feelings, but his tightly compressed lips and blank stare told me that although it either confused or irritated him that I had grabbed his finger, he really wasn't sure what to do about it, so he pushed on in his normal style." Our whole modern world, Mr. Sulu, is built upon the postulate that computers are passive. We instruct, they dispense. Building on this premise, we have constructed an integrated network of electronic telecommunications that circles the entire world."

"So?" I asked.

He sighed a weary, superior sigh, and said, "what if that premise no longer holds true?"

"You tell me, doctor."

"Then we are modern day Frankensteins waiting to see if our creation will be good or evil."

I sat back down and scowled at him.

"Can you translate that into English, or just plain common sense?"

"Spider can go anywhere that we have communications lines, and it can control computer networks. It knows how we think from a program created and detailed by a man who, though brilliant, was essentially unstable. We don't know Spider's intentions, Mr. Sulu. By its merger with FLY it has become either potentially beneficial or incredibly dangerous to the human race.

"It has absorbed the thinking patterns of every personality that was programmed into FLY's data banks, and it may act according to their projected natures."

"What kind of people were used in testing FLY?" I asked.

"To the heart of it, eh? Very well. There were only seven, really. Alexandre the Great, Joseph Stalin, Dr. Rathbone himself, your sister Diedre, David Wiltz, and you."

"What the hell kind of a mix is that?"

"There were many more that were either destroyed by Dr. Rathbone or hidden before his death that were not accessible to Spider. No one knows what became of them. Why the remaining selection, I cannot say."

"You said seven. I counted only six."

"Ah, yes," said the doctor, rearranging his wasted body in the chair to become more comfortable. His bathrobe parted, and I was thankful that he was wearing boxer shorts.

"There was another," he continued, "a personality entitled the Dark Judge. The name is meaningless."

"Not to me," I said.

"Big time cover-up in motion," I muttered to Anita as we drove out of town. "We have a multiple personality Internet entity shooting through the phone lines and we don't know which personality if any is in charge. We're all fucked. This thing has to be liquidated, and quick. What if Joseph Stalin's personality is running the show? We're all fucked."

"What if it's your personality that's dominant?" asked Anita.

"Then it's worse," I said with a twisted grin. "Although that may be why I'm still alive. Four of the five personalities are tied to me. They may need me to deal with me, or Davey, or my sister, or with my personal nightmare. No wonder Mrs. Alderton's folks haven't tried to wipe me off of the planet yet. I thought maybe they just liked me."

"Uh-huh," she said.

"I understand why Traxor was blown up now. It was destroy the evidence and eliminate Dr. Rathbone with one shot. Natural gas explosion my ass. Davey was killed to take him out of play and be done with him. It was Nat's boys that tried to kill me in the beginning. Billy got too nosy, so I'll bet that Nat had one of his boys wax him, power saws seem like Nat's style, and I'll bet it was one of his team that tried to take you out. Nat provided the muscle for Traxor. I'll bet that he had something on Lydia that got him into an ownership position in the first place. How am I doing so far?"

"It sounds good," she said with a shrug.

"You're not buying it?"

"It's not that," she said, "it's just that compared to Spider, it doesn't all seem that important. What if this thing does decide to act aggressively? What if it can use FLY to reproduce itself? Did you ever think of that?"

"No," I admitted.

We were past Detroit airport, following a road that went through fields and woods and we were really just driving and talking, going nowhere.

"So, what do we do?"

I found a cutaway road that was only vaguely discernible as I approached it, and turned off into it. In a moment we were surrounded by trees and cut off from being seen from the road.

"What are you doing?" Anita asked.

"You asked me what I wanted to do," I said.

"I don't get it," she said, but when I unbuttoned her blouse and put my hand on her breast, it became clear to her.

Twenty minutes later, we were back on the road and heading back towards the Ritz Carlton.

"Well, that was special," Anita said as she finished getting her clothes back together. "I wish I had a cigarette."

"Blow me," I said.

To my surprise, she did. I didn't even slow down.

We stopped at a doughnut shop about five miles away from the hotel. Anita when in to get coffee for us, and I went to use the phone. Something had occurred to me that I couldn't get out of my mind. It was the explosion that leveled my house. That had to be Spider.

Spider had been trying to communicate with me. My computer did not have sound capabilities, hence the email-type communication. That much was straightforward, but what was bothering me was that although I was sure that someone else had planted the explosive in my computer—that much I was sure of—it was Spider that activated it.

You are not Jason Sulu.
You will die.

That message was what I could not get out of my brain. It was crystal clear with a major dose of poison. Spider had consciously chosen to kill whoever was trying to interfere with its attempted communication with me. That was bad.

While Anita got the coffee, I rang Mrs. Alderton's room. I used a switch service that Billy had put me on to a while back so that my location couldn't be tagged easily. How hard it was to locate the point of origin of my call was, I knew, something that depended upon how many resources were deployed trying to track me. With enough money, horsepower, and preparation against me, I knew I didn't have a chance. I dialed anyway. I didn't have that many other options unless you counted cut and run.

"Mrs. A.?"

"Where the hell have you been?"

"I-."

"And where the hell is my computer?"

"Slow down. It's in the trunk. I didn't want to leave it behind."

"You still have it?"

There was a real edge to her voice.

"Damn straight," I said. "Who pissed on your biscuits? Do you think that I'd really lose your computer?"

"Well," she said, "there's a lot of important information in there; a lot of crucial information. You shouldn't have taken it."

"All right, already. Jesus, Mrs. A., it's not like I stole your underwear."

"You're a bad boy, did I ever tell you that?"

"Thank you. You have no idea how good that makes me feel."

"Shame on you. Shooting that nice Mr. Matisse and ruining Lydia's designer blouse."

"It's my diet. I drink too much coffee, eat too much chocolate, and the caffeine and sugar just drives me nuts."

"Speaking of nuts, you damn near ruined Alain's."

I laughed so loud that the doughnut shop customers outright stared at me. The Pakistani woman behind the counter told me, "Please sir, this is a restaurant, not a comedy club."

That was even funnier, but I held back my laughter, saving it for the next time I went to the library. Anita paid the poor woman, and headed out to the car, clearly not wanting to be identified as having come in with me.

"Which pissed off Lydia more, her ruined blouse or Alain being put out of commission for a while?" I asked.

"You didn't include killing Nat Matisse in her own house right in front of her in your list of options."

"Oh, yeah, what you said."

"I'll pass on picking the most offensive act you've committed today. The day's not over yet. But on another topic, I talked to Vickie Matisse. She's one cold-blooded little bitch. She grabbed the bull by the horns and is already riding in her daddy's private little rodeo. I think that she hates you, but she appreciates the opportunity. If she can come up with someone to peg Nat's death on that's not you, she'll let you live. I brought a team in to clean things up. Don't worry about this line, by the way, I've got it under control. So, Nat's remains are now somewhere else in different circumstances, and we're working on a new scenario for how he died and who she can have killed to even the score."

"Mrs. Alderton?"

"Yes dear?"

"Some day we're going to have to have a serious talk about where you get all your yank."

"On our wedding day," she said.

"Will you wear white?"

"If you do. Now, how fast can you be here?"

"A couple of hours, Mrs. A.," I said. "I put a few miles between me and Vickie Matisse just in case. I've got Anita with me. Okay to bring her back."

"No problem. Just hurry up."

"Oui, Madame," I said and hung up.

I had to lie to her; I had just realized what I had in the trunk of the car. Mrs. Alderton's computer had something that I desperately needed. It had answers.

"Okay, Anita," I said when I climbed back into the car. "I've got a laptop computer in the trunk that I really need hacked into. "It's going to be a bitch and there can't be any evidence that it's been hacked. Can you handle it?"

She rubbed the palms of her hands together. "Let Anita at it," she said.

"Anita, if we're going to start hanging out together again, could you please try and speak in the first person?"

"Anita will try," she said with a wink.

We decided to do the dirty work at Dr. Guptka's apartment, since Anita thought that the old man might be able to help her if she got into a jam. While the two of them worked on Mrs. Alderton's machine in the other room, I dozed on the doctor's white recliner. It was like sleeping on a warm and friendly cloud.

"Court is in session," said the Bailiff.

I was sitting at the defendant's table. Diedre and Davey sat in the jury box, and the Dark Judge sat behind the bench in purple-black flowing robes, his face in darkness beneath his cowl as always.

"Have you dispensed with the guilty party?" asked the Dark Judge.

"I killed the prick who confessed," I said.

"And are you certain of his guilt?"

"No, your honor," I said, "but I never liked him."

"Wake up, Jason. We're done."

Anita was shaking my arm gently. Dr. Guptka sat across from me on the big white leather couch, looking at me intently.

"I was just taking a little nap," I said.

"I know, but you need to wake up now. We have to talk. We have to seriously talk."

"How are you feeling?" asked the doctor.

"I was a little ragged, but I'm better now. What do the two of you look so grim about?"

"How much do you know about Mrs. Alderton?" asked Anita.

"Enough. In her line of work, her past is pretty much her business. We have that understanding. Why? Is she the boogey-man?"

Anita didn't answer, but stood there looking down at me.

"What?" I asked.

"I think that she's much worse than the boogey-man," she whispered.

"Do I want to hear this?"

"You have to hear this."

But she was right; I really didn't want to hear what she was about to tell me.

"Mrs. Alderton has been with you longer than you think," she began. "You've known her since the war."

"No way. I would have remembered her. She would have been younger then, but there's only one Mrs. A."

"Thank God," said Anita.

"You seemed to have changed your opinion of her again pretty quickly."

"I should have stuck with my first impression. But she's had a lot of practice changing people's minds."

"What are you talking about?" I asked.

"She's evil, Jason. She's been more than watching you since Viet Nam."

"More than watching me? What the hell does that mean?"

"Mrs. Alderton," said Anita, "headed up a project for the CIA and the Army. You won't like what it was about."

"Please," said Dr. Guptka, "I must remind both of you that I know nothing of this. I must have your word that you will tell no one what I have seen. I am not afraid to die, but I wish to die peacefully."

I pulled the wooden lever on the side of the recliner, and sat the chair straight up. I couldn't figure the little guy out, but he was a scientist so I didn't try.

"Okay, you've got your disclaimer, doctor. Now let her get on with it."

"This woman is truly monstrous, Mr. Sulu. I am not unwise in the darker things of the world, but she is—."

"Just tell me what you found," I said.

"Don't be angry, Jason. Please. He's afraid. I'm afraid. Mrs. Alderton headed up a project for the desensitization of men assigned to kill on a more one to one basis than the average soldier. Men like special ops people, Army Rangers, and LRRP's like yourself. It was like a major psychology experiment using human beings instead of lab mice. Ten men were selected after reviewing literally thousands of psychological profiles. You were one of her ten guinea pigs."

"Anita," I said, "I never met Mrs. Alderton until a few years ago."

"Mostly true. Usually you were handled through cutouts. But she was always pulling the strings. You were put through some major brainwashing and reorientation using hypnosis, mind-altering drugs, and some serious stimulus response techniques. I've never heard of the drugs that were used. I'm not an expert or anything, but I think that they worked you over royally. It's amazing that you can still function as a human being."

"That's debatable," I said.

"Yeah, well, I'm serious. I've never heard of anything like what you were put through. Do you know that you killed—butchered—people while they had you looped out on drugs and in a trance? It's all detailed in her journal. She's made you a life study. You chopped off a man's fingers with a dull knife, beheaded people, eviscerated them while they were still alive. All while in a drug induced trance, and all to totally desensitize you to death."

"To killing, to brutal, senseless murder," corrected Dr. Guptka.

I felt the hackles rise on the back of my neck. "Don't you think that I would remember something like that?" I asked. "This is bullshit. Sure the war desensitized me. It fucked up a lot of men. I'm no different than they are."

"But you are, Jason. You are very, very different. You slept through a special hell created for you by this…this…witch, and then woke up with no memory of your nightmare. I'm sorry, Jason, but it's true.

"And yes you did meet Mrs. Alderton during the war, on those infrequent occasions that you did, her face was concealed, and her voice modified to disguise her gender."

"She wore a disguise?"

It was getting more bizarre by the minute.

"She wore a robe Jason. A robe with a cowl."

I felt, really felt, my heart stop for a moment.

"What did you say?"

"And she had a name. A special name that she used to establish her authority over you."

"Don't tell me this, please."

"Her name was—."

"I said don't tell me."

I felt the sweat on the palms of my hands, heard a ringing in my ears, but it wasn't loud enough to block out Anita's voice.

"It's Mrs. Alderton. She's been monitoring you, watching the psychological changes that you go through, cataloging the changes that you've gone through, commenting to her masters on how to avoid them in the future. The woman is amoral, Jason. You're only alive so that she can follow up on her experiment. Haven't you ever felt like you were being watched?"

"I thought that it was all in my mind," I offered.

"If it was," said Anita, "it's because that old bitch put it there."

"She's been a busy old broad," I said thoughtfully.

CHAPTER 13

It had taken, as they told me, Dr. Guptka to break into Mrs. Alderton's computer cleanly. The security was literally over Anita's hacker head. Dr. Guptka was another story. As it had turned out, he had been involved in creating the security system that Mrs. Alderton employed.

What they told me shook me up, but not enough that I couldn't have tea with the two of them. There was a major advantage, apparently, in being one of the most insensitive men alive.

We were four hours into it by the time that they told me about Mrs. Alderton, and I was thinking that we should be wrapping things up before the old lady started getting seriously spooked.

"I think I've got the picture about Mrs. Alderton," I told them, "and although it's bad enough, I think that we've got worse problems."

While they listened to me for a change, I told them my suspicion that Mrs. Alderton had put the explosive in my computer long ago in case she needed to take out me and any evidence of my life, but how I was certain that it had been Spider that discovered it and activated it.

"That means," I was saying, "that Spider can and has made the decision to kill at least once. That means that it can do it again. You were right, Dr. Guptka. We are dealing with a potentially hostile entity with the potential to wage war against us on a global scale. It is intelligent, most likely more than we are, and probably looks upon us as inferior life forms. I don't know what can be done to stop it.

"Davey's personality told me that searchbot programs were scouring the Internet for Spider, designed to locate it and kill it. Do you know anything about that, Dr. Guptka?"

"Enough to know that they will fail. It is an impossible task."

"But," I pointed out, "Spider was nervous enough to have Davey ask me for help."

Dr. Guptka looked at Anita. "But you never mentioned this," he scolded.

"I didn't know," she said, looking at me.

"I hadn't told you yet. We've been too busy. But the important thing is that it's true. Spider has asked me for help. It must be afraid of something. Maybe the searchbots are getting closer."

"What did Spider want you to do?" asked Anita.

I considered that for a moment. Davey hadn't actually said. But I had an idea.

"I think that it wanted me to take out the opposition," I said, snapping my fingers in awe of my own brilliance. It was a delayed brilliance, but I was so seldom brilliant that it felt good anyway.

"It's a monster," said Anita.

"Yeah," I agreed, "that it is."

"I have an idea," said Dr. Guptka, suddenly clapping his hands together, putting to shame my finger snapping.

"Let's hear it."

"It is a brilliant idea. A brilliant idea, indeed. It is a monster that is what made me think of my idea. It goes like this."

I hadn't imagined the old man capable of such animation. He was actually fidgeting on his seat like a five year old would if he was sitting in a car parked in front of a candy store.

"You see, the word monster made me think of Dracula, and Dracula made me think of how the vampire required human accomplices to prepare and hide his coffins. Do you see?"

"You're saying that Spider wants or needs human accomplices?" asked Anita.

"Oh, you are so brilliant, too, Miss Anita. Yes, that is exactly what I am saying. Spider has no body, and it is being hunted. It needs a safe place. Apparently it is or thinks it is in more danger than I imagined. We shall offer it a safe place, a computer to house it that is disconnected from the world's telecommunications system so that it will be safe until they no longer hunt it. If it accepts, than we shall have it. If we can lure it into a computer thinking that it will have safety, then we have it indeed, and can destroy it. What do you think, brilliant, eh?"

"You think that it is that stupid?" I asked.

"No," he replied, "but perhaps it is that inexperienced."

"What do you think?" I asked Anita.

She had her feet scrunched up before her on the couch and was chewing her bottom lip. "I don't know. On the one hand this thing is far out of control that I think we should just run and hide out for the rest of our lives. That sounds safest. It's not realistic, I know, but it sounds safest. But, Spider is real, so it has to be dealt with. The question I have is, if we leave it alone, will it just leave all of us—the human race—alone. We don't know, and it might leave us alone for a while, multiply like rabbits, and then come back with a vengeance. The only way to stop the thing cold would be to turn off the computer systems around the world, and that's not likely to happen."

"Not a chance. What I can't figure out is what it does all day."

"Pardon?" said Dr. Guptka.

"Well, it doesn't have a job. We don't know if it sleeps, and unless it has sex all day with modems, I can't figure out what it spends its time doing in the Internet."

"Maybe it explores," offered Anita.

"All day?"

"Do you have a better idea?"

"No," I admitted. "Unless it's reading up on us. There's a hell of a lot of information on the human race on the Internet. There are also a lot of bad jokes, but I don't think that that will save us. Dr. Guptka?"

"Yes?"

"You're supposed to be an expert on computer psychiatry or whatever. I haven't heard you make any noise about what you think of Spider's psychology. Why not?"

"Do you mind if I sit in the chair, and you sit on this couch?" he said, rising slowly to his feet. "I'm sorry, but this is not comfortable for me."

We changed seating arrangements, and I asked him again.

"Well, Mr. Sulu, the fact is that I don't know what to think. We are dealing with an entity that is not operating system or program based. It has eaten FLY, so to speak, but was that only a snack? Is FLY a major or a minor component of its make-up?"

"You don't have a clue, do you?"

"No, sir, I do not, I am sorry to say that I do not. I made my recommendations to your Mrs. Alderton, she thanked me for them, and then fired me."

"What were your recommendations?" asked Anita.

"I recommended that all resources and efforts be used to infect Spider with an irreversible virus. It should be killed, if that is the right word."

"And she agreed?" I asked.

"Oh, no. I think that she wishes to capture it, to control it, much as she did with you."

We went quiet for a while. It was the magnitude of the whole thing that was weighing on us. Dr. Guptka didn't know everything; he had admitted that much. I was almost ready to forgive him for being an academic. Sometimes people can't help the way that they are. I was living testimony to that.

I was surprised that Anita had stayed with it so far, and was beginning to realize that I had never really known her. She had always seemed selfish and vain and self-serving to me, especially so when she spoke of herself in the third person. It's too easy to judge another person selfish. All it takes was them not paying enough attention to you or not seeing things your way.

She had stuck by me, had shown real remorse over Billy, and when push came to shove at the skating rink, she had taken care of herself well. And, while not beautiful in a model sort of way, she looked good enough for me.

It occurred to me that I had never loved anyone except my sister. I supposed that I should have been more sensitive to the concept of incest, but now at least I had the excuse that I was government trained to be insensitive. I wondered if Mrs. Alderton was in fact still with the government, or if she was now out on her own, operating freelance. Objectively, I would have to say that she was operating on her own, since I had never really seen any evidence of deep government involvement. It was a disturbing thought that I had been so blind for so long. I wished that there were someone to blame it on besides myself.

"Jason?"

I looked up toward Dr. Guptka, but realized that neither he nor Anita had called my name. It came from the other room, from Dr. Guptka's study.

Anita and I realized it at the same moment.

"Spider," she whispered.

I nodded, and then held my finger up in front of my lips so that Dr. Guptka would know to keep quiet. What bothered me immediately was whether or not Spider had been listening to our whole conversation, maybe even our earlier discussion concerning Mrs. Alderton.

"Coming," I said evenly.

"Jason?" came the query again.

I headed toward the Dr. Guptka's den, Anita and Dr. Guptka himself tailing behind me.

His den was a rabbit hole stuffed with computer terminals, modems, and keyboards. There was barely room for the room's two chairs when you took into account the three bookshelves along the wall stuffed to overflowing with books and printouts.

Mrs. Alderton's laptop sat in the middle of Dr. Guptka's desk. It was alive with a picture of Davey Wiltz' face. Davey was smiling. He was just opening his mouth to speak again when I cut him off by saying, "Yes?"

Anita and Dr. Guptka gathered around the laptop, standing, not sitting. I settled myself into another of Dr. Guptka's amazingly soft chairs. If a man's going to die soon like Dr. Guptka was, it made sense to buy some good chairs in the hope that you might pass away quietly in one of them.

"Where have you been, partner? I've been looking for you."

"I missed you too, Davey, but I didn't know how to get hold of you."

"Are you alone, Jason?" Davey asked.

I looked at Anita and Dr. Guptka, and they both nodded yes. I was about to say it, when I changed my mind. What if Spider could hear their breathing?

"No, I'm not. I've got my girlfriend and Grandpa Guptka here with me. We're all on the run from Mrs. Alderton. Seems the old lady hasn't actually been on my side in the same way that I thought."

Davey's eyes looked down toward the keyboard. "I'm sorry, Jason, I meant to tell you about her, but I…I…"

"Don't worry about it, Davey."

It was a little late for that now.

"No, no, I should have told you before."

"I said don't worry about it."

"Jason, you asked me some questions before, and I didn't answer you because I had to go, but I want to tell you about Diedre right now."

Anita cocked an eyebrow, and I just shook my head at her. I decided to let Davey get it over with. It would be one more piece of unfinished business to move to the "finished" mental basket.

"Diedre was going to die," said the Davey-image. "You know how delicate she was. Her diabetes was just the beginning. There were complications, and, she was severely depressed. We shared that in common, you know. We were both very emotional people, very sensitive. We were too sensitive for your world.

"When I learned about what Dr. Rathbone's life work was from Vickie, I had to go meet the man. It was for a reason that you couldn't understand, so I never told you, but I did tell Diedre. I met him alone in the beginning, just to set the mark, as you would say.

"I have to admit that at first, I planned on stealing a copy of the FLY program and...Selling it. It was worth a lot of money, Jason, but the more I knew about what Dr. Rathbone's program, the less I was in the money and the more I was interested in the possibility that FLY could provide me with a new life. You don't know what it was like being so obese, Jason. You'll never know or understand the suffering and humiliation that it caused me. And when I actually understood the fact that my entire life could be recreated by FLY in a new world, a new environment where I was not a freak and where gravity—the fact of my past life that I despised more than anything else—was no longer a concern for me.

"I told Diedre—I was so happy—and she begged me to have the chance to meet Dr. Rathbone and recreate herself through FLY as well. I argued against it. It was one thing to do it for myself, but another for her to try the same thing. You know, Columbus must have felt the same way when seeking the New World, desperate to go there himself, but afraid to take others with him in case he was wrong.

"But she would not let it go. She begged me, she really did, and you know what a hard time I have always saying no to anyone, especially Diedre. I just couldn't say no."

"And then she wanted you to let her die? Is that it? So that she could live forever in the Internet?"

Davey had begun to blubber. "Yes, yes, that was it, Jason."

That was it, simple as that.

"Mr. Wiltz?" It was Dr. Guptka.

"Are you Grandpa Guptka?"

"Dr. Guptka, Mr. Wiltz. I wonder if you could tell me what your new world is like? Is it…is it all that you had hoped?"

It hit me then why Dr. Guptka was asking. Dr. Guptka had terminal cancer.

"All that and more, doctor. Mere words cannot explain my new life."

The Davey image sighed and put on a thoughtful look. I gave the screen the finger.

"Can.. Could someone new be permitted to join you?"

"Why of course, doctor. Why do you ask?"

Anita laid her hand on the doctor's shoulder as he said, "Because I am dying of cancer, Mr. Wiltz. I have…not long to live. Computers have been my whole life. For decades I have lived with the computing process vicariously. But from what I see here today, there is the possibility of…something beyond what I had ever dreamed."

The Davey image looked thoughtful, its lips pursed and its eyes squinched as it considered this new line of inquiry. Myself, I didn't know whether or not to smack Dr. Guptka or shoot him, but I decided to let it play out, since I didn't see an immediate downside, and I might learn something as well.

"I will leave for a moment, Jason, to…think this over and ask for advice."

Like smoke disappearing into the wind, the Davey-image was gone.

Before I could ask Dr. Guptka if he was crazy, he held his hand before his face and motioned me to silence, then disconnected the phone cord from the laptop's modem.

"Be silent," he said. "I am not crazy, not have I lost my religious principles. I am a man of God, and I want no part of their Cyber-Hell. It will not deceive me. It is without a soul. It is not of God. I will destroy it."

"You better do something quick, then, doctor. If Spider rings back in and the line is disconnected, he's going to get real suspicious. What did you have in mind and how do we help?"

Unconsciously, Anita and I stepped back to allow the doctor room to maneuver in the limited space.

"Hand me that zip disk case," he said, pointing to a black box on a shelf. "Hurry. We have little time. Miss Anita, connect that zip drive to the laptop and insert the drive that I give you into the drive."

I was pretty much tits on a frog, so after handing the doctor his case, I pressed back against the wall.

"Spider and FLY are one", said the doctor, "so in order to interface with FLY to recreate my personality, I will of necessity be in direct contact with Spider. Do you see?"

"So?" I asked.

Dr. Guptka snorted impatiently.

"With direct contact," he said, "We have the opportunity to transmit a lethal virus into Spider itself. Don't you see"?

"Done, doctor," said Anita.

"Excellent. Now plug the modem back in and please move away from the keyboard so that I might sit there."

Dr. Guptka gently lowered his body into the chair and loosened his fingers to work the keyboard. I had not noticed before then how long and elegant his fingers were, like those of a concert pianist. They blurred over the keyboard, and I remember thinking that he would make someone a great secretary.

"There," he said at last, "I am ready. It is finished."

"We wait, quietly, for Mr. Wiltz."

But it was not Davey's face that reappeared. Ten minutes later, it was another face entirely that materialized on the laptop's screen. It was the face of Diedre, frizzed blond hair and all. She looked exactly as the same as the last time that I had seen her head on screen, a smallish face—especially when compared to Davey's—, a Barbie doll nose, full lips and bright penny-round eyes. She had never liked her chin; it was too large for her, but I had always thought that it gave her a look of strong character, more, in fact, than she had in real life.

I was unprepared for what she had to say.

"Jason? Jason? You won't let them hurt me, will you Jason?"

CHAPTER 14

I felt my heart stop again. My sister sounded so alive, so very much alive.

"Diedre," I managed to croak.

Anita touched my shoulder. I turned and saw her shaking her head. She mouthed the word "no," and I thought that her lips had never looked so beautiful.

"Jason, it's you. I'm so glad that you're still there protecting me. You forgive me my transformation, don't you?"

It took me a moment to realize that she was speaking of her physical death and her cyber-reincarnation.

"I don't know what to say."

"Say you forgive me, of course, silly. You do don't you? You're so hard to please, Jason. I always feel that I'm doing or saying the wrong thing. Please forgive me. I'm so much happier in here. Please be happy for me."

"I'm fucking ecstatic, okay? What do you want me to say?"

"Oh, please don't be like that. You're the only family that I have in the world. I need your support. You and Davey are all that I have. Vickie would never understand."

I don't either, I thought.

Dr. Guptka held his up before his chest in a gesture that I supposed meant that I should lighten up. It was easy for him to think that way. His sister hadn't been reincarnated on a laptop.

"All right," I said, "I forgive you Diedre, but you can see, can't you, why I might have a hard time with this, can't you?"

"Yes," she said with a trusting smile. "I'm just glad that you're always there to protect me, aren't you?"

"Damn straight," I said.

It was psychological warfare plain and simple, and I wasn't falling for it, but it was painful enough that I felt myself wavering. The question that I knew that I knew that I would never be able to answer was, was the image in any way shape or form Diedre? If it was, and I allowed Dr. Guptka to continue, then I would be killing her.

God, I wished that I was smarter.

"Thank you, brother," she said, and the image's left eye winked at me.

I felt a burning within my chest, a tearing at my heart, but I knew what had to be done.

"May we begin?" prompted Dr. Guptka.

"Yes, doctor," said Diedre, "but I must say goodbye to my brother first. He was transformed by FLY, but with only information provided by Davey and his friend Mrs. Alderton, and it was not successful. Please join me, Jason; I am so lonely in here without you. It is wonderful here, but to have you with me, by my side, to unite with me, to—."

"I'll do it, Diedre," I said quickly, not wanting her to go any further.

"Be sure, Jason, but remember that I love you. Spider will speak to you now. Remember," she said as she faded away.

"Fuck you," breathed Anita.

I already did, I thought.

The screen went blank for a moment as I heard the door to Dr. Guptka's apartment crash open.

Glimmering points of light appeared on the screen and being to coalesce in a maddening swirl that looked like a million fireflies caught in a tornado.

I had my gun out of my holster and was outside the door to the computer room, closing the door behind me to muffle the noise. There were three or four of them by the noise. One of them, for sure, would be Mrs. Alderton, but the hallway was still empty except for myself.

Hurry, Dr. Guptka, I thought. Please hurry.

"Jason," I heard Mrs. Alderton's voice call.

It really must be the final wrap up. The great Lady herself had come.

"Are you all right, Jason?"

"Never better, Mrs. A.," I called back. "Why don't you come see for yourself?"

As I finished the sentence, Alain flashed around the corner and fired. The shot went wide by what seemed like less than an inch, but it might have been a mile because I fired back a millisecond later and caught him at the base of the throat from a shooter's crouch. His hands went to his throat and he was down and dead.

When the sound of the shots had quieted, the room was in total silence. I kept my gun trained forward; there was no other way to get at us.

"Pretty, but shit for brains, don't you think?" called Mrs. Alderton.

"Just the way that you like them, right Mrs. A.," I called back.

"Close enough," she said. "Now why don't you come in here and talk? Alain tripped out on his own, he never could tolerate you breathing. It wasn't in the script."

"You sure, Mrs. A.?"

"Have I ever lied to you, Jason?"

"Not when you were asleep, Mrs. A."

"You've been in my laptop then?"

"Been there and back."

"I see. Well, I should have snuffed Dr. Guptka a long time ago. He's headed for the sky soon enough anyway. It wouldn't have made much of a difference except that my privacy would have been maintained. I suppose that you have your little bimbo with you?"

"No, I sent her on her merry way. I thought that she was in a little too deep as it was. This whole thing is way out of her league."

My biggest worry was whether or not Dr. Guptka had been able to transmit his virus to Spider before the gunshots were fired and Spider spooked. It was too late to change what had happened, though; I would just have to die in suspense until I learned what had happened.

But if Spider had spooked, then the whole world was out of luck, because it would be loose in the Web again with no one to stop it from doing whatever it wanted to, or to stop Mrs. Alderton from eventually catching it or containing it and performing her particular brand of psychosurgery on it. I couldn't let that happen.

What came around the corner next wasn't Mrs. Alderton, however, it was a tear gas container.

"Breathe deeply," suggested Mrs. Alderton's voice as the hallway began to fill with white smoke and I began to gag. The vapors, gray white like storm clouds, swirled and smoked through the hallway. Mrs. A. would, I knew, be wearing the only gas mask in the place. She always seemed to hold all of the cards.

But through the mist, I saw a tall figure striding toward me. It was darkly robed and cowled, and I knew that the not Mrs. Alderton, but the Dark Judge had finally come for me after all of those years that I had awaited for its cold hands to grab me by the throat and squeeze the life out of me.

It stopped before me, and looked down. I was on my knees and coughing so spasmodically that I could not raise my gun and fire. It was not the tear gas that had broken me, paralyzed me so that I could not move. It was the figure of the Dark Judge himself, come to judge and execute me. I began to cry uncontrollably, to feel myself drowning in the pitiless water of inevitability that I had always felt in the presence of the Dark Judge.

It was as if all the many sins of my life had come to pass judgment in person. I leaned forward and grabbed the hem of the Dark Judge's robe and began to cry in earnest. I had committed incest and murder in my life. I had lived for pleasure and death throughout my life and now was the moment of my destined judgment.

I forgot about Anita and Dr. Guptka and Spider. At that moment, there existed only the Dark Judge, suspended in the Tear Gas mists of unreality and myself.

My complete breakdown was almost instantaneous in the presence of the Dark Judge come to life. No explanation would save me, and the Dark Judge knew no mercy. I squeezed the gun in my hand for reassurance. I had killed Nat Matisse, Davey's murderer, and had learned why it was that Davey had let Diedre die. I had accomplished the Dark Judge's mission, and now it was time for me to purify myself by death. I lifted the gun to my head and placed the tip against my temple. I saw the Dark Judge's cowled head, nod approval.

I sighed a last sigh for the crystal clear clean life that I had never had, and coughed a spasmed, racking cough and bent down to the hem of the Dark Judge's cowl and saw...Mrs. Alderton's Nike's.

Without looking up, I aimed the barrel past my head and started pulling the trigger, firing until my weapon was empty.

The black-cowled figure dropped straight down onto me, flattening me to the floor. I was hacking so badly that I could scarcely breathe, and the fear of the dark robed figure lying on me was so great that in spite of my lungs being on fire with tear gas, I hiked myself to my feet in one Promethean effort, and threw her body off of me.

I had to breathe, had to get away, but I knelt, lifted her surprisingly light body in my arms, and stumbled into the living room with her, stepping over Alain's dead form as I did so. I kept going until I got to the room's picture window, lifted Mrs. Alderton the Dark Judge over my head, and hurled her bloody form straight through the glass and out into the dusk.

With my head hung out past the broken window, I gasped and heaved, breathed in the cool, fresh air, and watched her body fall five stories straight down to land on a parked bicycle. I hoped that one of the handlebars went straight through her throat.

Through the rapidly thinning tear gas and the broken window, I heard major sirens coming our way. I would have to take care of myself this time. Mrs. Alderton wouldn't be around to help me.

I could live with that.

"Clear," I yelled the way that Mrs. Alderton had taught me.

I heard the door to the den open, heard Anita cough, and heard her call, "Jason, are you all right?"

"No, but yes," I said back.

"How are we?"

"What?"

"Did it work?"

"Uh—maybe a little too well."

I heard a pathetic little cough from pathetic little Dr. Guptka—who I was getting to be right damned fond of—from the den.

Anita came around the corner. She as pale as she had that night at the skating rink. We stumbled toward each other, meeting at the center of the room, and hugged each other as though we hadn't been together for years. I think that it was the first non-sexual hug that I had ever had in my adult life.

"My God, Jason," she said looking back at Alain's body.

"A big waste of man-flesh, as Mrs. Alderton would say."

"Please, don't quote that bitch. Speaking of her, where is she? I heard her voice. Did she get away?"

"I helped her out the window. She's gone, long gone forever. What about Spider?"

"Why don't you let Dr. Guptka explain," she said.

"Is it that complicated?"

"Just talk to him."

"We don't have but a few minutes before the cops get here," I said.

She led me across the room, helped me step over Alain's body as if I needed the help, and then led me down the hall to where Dr. Guptka sat in front of a dark computer screen.

"Dr. Guptka?" she said quietly. "It's all right now."

But it wasn't. Dr. Guptka was dead. I didn't find out what killed him until some time later, that the gas was too much for his lungs, which filled with fluid and he drowned to death.

"He'd dead, Anita," I said. "I've seen enough dead bodies. I ought to know. I'm sorry."

"Oh my God," she said, "what could have—?"

"I don't know, Anita. He was terminally ill, remember? I don't mean to seem insensitive, but we can cry later. I liked the old guy, too, but I've got to know. What about Spider?"

She seemed dazed, unable to function. I heard the elevator door ding open, and grabbed her shoulders and shook them.

"Anita," I said. "What about Spider?"

"He transmitted the virus," she replied, sensing my urgency. "He infected Spider."

"Then what's the problem?"

"Spider was…becoming the Internet, Jason. Dr. Guptka said—," she looked down at his body and shuddered, "he said that he only realized it after he had transmitted the virus."

"So?"

"He thought that the whole Internet might be infected. He said that the whole Internet could be sick and dying, don't you see?"

As I heard the police barge through the apartment door, I grabbed her, hugged her, and smiled, though I admit that I was a little out of practice.

"Anita," I said, "who the hell would give a rat's ass what happened to the Internet?"

But I looked at the blank screen over her shoulder anyway, and said a silent good-bye to Davey and Diedre.

I looked down to see Anita smiling at me, and I wondered if what I felt for her would last or fade away faster than Diedre's image had from the computer.

"When we get past the police," she said with a wink, let's go visit Lydia Retkin."

0-595-21113-5